Dear "Herm"

— with a cast of dozens

by

Leo Rosten

McGRAW-HILL BOOK COMPANY
New York   St. Louis   San Francisco
Sydney   Düsseldorf   Mexico   Panama
London   Toronto

Book design by Marcy J. Katz

123456789BABA7987654

Library of Congress Cataloging in Publication Data

Rosten, Leo Calvin, date
Dear "Herm," with a cast of dozens.

    I. Title.
PZ3.R7386De [PS3535.07577]   813'.5'2   73-16226
ISBN 0—07—053981—2

To
my readers

Contents

Lament
for an
Unlisted Number

Cinderella LAMINATED SHIMS

83 Wacker Drive
Chicago, Illinois 60612

Jan. 16

Leo Rosten
Apt. 39-A
Vesuvius Towers
644 E. 68 St.
New York, N.Y. 10021

Dear Leo:

I bet you will be knocked for a <u>Loop</u> (and I
do not mean the Loop in downtown Chi.—which as you
know, being a former native of, enjoys World-Wide
Fame) to hear from a H.S. class-mate after all these
many years, your old buddy Herman P. Klitcher, or
"Herm" as I prefer it from true pals of old. Do you
remember me?

I even bet you are wondering, "Why in carnation is Hermie Klitcher writing me? Is he hard up
for dough—which, if he puts the bite on me, he can
just go to % # ! & ! ! "

Well, don't worry, kiddo. I am making a bun-
dle as Asst. Mid-West Sales Mgr. of the Company
above you.

This missive, to be absolutely frank and
honest about it, is the idea of my wife "Flo"
(which is short for Florence) who you never had the
pleasure of meeting. And here is why. All of us in the

Klitcher house are big TV fans, so last night as we
are watching the Tube what name pops up in front of
our very eyes, after "Screenplay by" (at the end of
a movie we were watching) but—"LEO ROSTEN!"

I tell you, Leo, I cheered like you just made
the winning touchdown in the last 5 seconds in the
Rose Bowl!! So my wife Flo said "Say, Hermy, is that
not the fellow from Crane Tech High you went to
school with and have told me so much about?"

"It sure is," I grin.

Flo gives me her "O, yeh?" look, with those
B.B. eyes she uses whenever she smells a put-
on and cracks "Okay, Lover, then how about you asking him for advice about You-Know-What?" (on account of our youngest kid Hortense, age 12, being in
the room).

"I sure will," I snap. And as soon as our
4 kids hit the sack, I telephone Long Distance to
N.Y.

Well, Leo, let me lay it on the line—you are
one H--- of a hard guy to get hold of!! Phone-wise, I
mean. I tried to call you maybe 10 times all of last
week-end (about this problem Flo and me have run
into). But those Info. Operators in N.Y. kept telling me you have an "Unlisted Number"—which makes
anyone trying to get a person with such a number go
nuts!

So I get a swell idea—and put in "Person-
to-Person" calls to every "Rosten" baring your
name in the Manhattan Phone Directory! Because I
figure this will not cost me 1-cent until I get you
in person, right? But I have to tell you that the results of what transpired were just disgusting!!

"Why?" you must be asking.

Well, I will tell you why.

The first "Rosten" I tell the Operator to

call (Person-to-Person) answers in a male's voice
like a couple of Frogs crawling through gravel "I
am getting sick-and-tired of being woke up at 11
P.M.!—" (I have to admit I forgot that in N.Y. you
are 1 hour later than we are in Chi., on account of
the way the sun hits your town before it moves over to
ours) "—by screw-balls demanding to know if I am
Leo Rosten, when my name is clearly printed in the
Manhattan phone book as Gustave!!!" (His name was
Gustave Rosten.) Wham, he hangs up so hard he must of
bust the part of the phone you hang up with.

The next "Rosten" owning a similar name
to you answers the next P-to-P Operator (who I had
plenty of trouble understanding, her accent being
from Jamaica or some other African republic). "No,
operator, my name is not Leo Rosten, and you have
woke me up just as I was falling asleep under the
spell of 2 Sleep-Eze pills. So kindly give whoever
is calling me this message: "Drop dead!""

The third "Rosten" on the list gets me a
hollow "That line has been dis-connected . . ."—
from a recording that sounds like a rowbot with a
hoarse muffler.

The #4 "Rosten" does not answer at all, so
I figure you are out at some fancy restaurant or
Literary Affair, being a big-time Author.

But the fifth "Rosten" has a very sweet
and friendly type voice (and I think "Thank God,")
which says "I am not named "Leo Rosten"! being a
female, but I have a cousin who is named "Leon
Rosten" if that would be of any help."

I sure jumped to grab at that straw, it being
the first to come along after 4 straight strike-
outs. "Okay, Operator, okay," I hurry "I will
talk to that party,"—because frankly, Leo, I think

maybe your whole name is "Leon" but you use "Leo"
for short, the way many a "Richard" is "Dick" or
like that. "Hello, Miss or Mrs. as the case may be"
I cry. "Can you give me the phone number for your
cousin as I am very eager to reach him?"

"Do you want "Leon Rosten's" number?"
croons the female voice.

"I do not want Paul Reveres," I retort.

"Okey-dokey" the broad answers "Just
hold the line as I go get it."

"I am on Long Distance!" I holler.

"So am I" she flips.

"That is true" I admit "so please step on
it!"

Well, pal, about $3.40 later that dum
bimbo returns to the line and says (so help me)
"Hel-lo?"

"Hello," I utter.

"Are you still there?" she warbels.

"I have not departed for Siam!"

"Do you have a pencil and paper handy?"

"I _always_ have a pencil and paper handy!"
I remind her "especially when calling Long Distance!"

"Then take down my cousin "Leon's" number—and if you do reach him—Are you planning to
phone him _right now?_"

"Why do you think I am calling?!" I
squawk.

"Well, give him my regards— "

"I will, I will!"

"My name is Belinda—B-E-L-I- not E! but
I-"

"Je-_zus_, O.K., What—is—his—number?!"
I demand.

"—and ask him is it not about time I heard
1 word from him, even a _postal card_, after 2 years or
maybe 3—"

"For crying' out _loud!_" I exclaim "Just
give me that number before I have to file for Bank-
rupcy!!"

"Oh, that is funny," that kook laughs and
laughs like she is trying out for a part on the Rowan
and Martin Show after they lost Goldie Kahn to the
movies.

"That laugh alone has set me back 2 more
bucks," I strangle. "Lady, _please_ just give me
the number—"

"I am sorry. I forgot you are calling
from—say, where _are you_ calling from?"

"Chicago," I explode.

"Chicago, Illinois?" she amazes.

"Chicago has been in Illinois ever since
the Declaration of Independents!"

"Oh, I just _love_ Chicago" she moans, and
the dawn comes on me that this muff is stinko, "That
Lake-front is a _dream,_ and the Wriggely Building is
so clean and beautiful I cry every time I think of
it."

"Belinda" I fume "if you do not give me
that number right _now_ I swear to God I will—"

"Wait a _minute_," she growls. "Are you a
Communist or something, taking the name of the Lord in
vein?"

"No, no, I'm sorry, I take that back. I
just—want—your—cousin's—number—"

"How do I know you are _on the level_?" she
pops from left field. "Why you could be a crook, or
in blackmail or some profession of that type. I do
not go around handing out my cousin Leon's telephone

number to every Tom, Dick and Jerry. So please i-den-
tify your self. By name! Hic! And occupration!"

Well, Leo, I grit all my teeth together
until my gums hurt, but respond as calmily as anyone
in my position can "My name is Herman P. Klitcher,
and I—"

"Herman what?" She squeals like she is
seeing the Grand Canon or a 2-headed kangaroo for the
first time.

"Herman Klitcher!" I seeth.

"You have to be kiddin!" she giggels.

"I do not!"

"Kolicher?" she gurgels.

"No, Klitcher!"

"With a "C"?" that tomato gives me.

"No, with—a—"K"!" I foam.

"I never heard of anyone called "Klincher" she huffs.

"It is not "Klincher" I protest. "It is
Klitcher"!" And I even spell it out for her, Leo.
"K-l-i-t-c-h-e-r!""

"That certainly is a strange name" she
meditates.

"I cannot help it!" I croak "That happens
to be the name I was born with,"

"No one is born with a name, wise guy. You
are handed one!"

"I was handed "Herman" but inherited
"Klitcher"!" I snort.

"Is that a German or Polish-type name?"
this ding-dong tortures me "or are you making it
up?!"

"It is of Litvak derivation and I am not
making it up!" I shout. "Check it for yourself!
Just look in the Suburbs-of-Chicago phone book!"

"Where do you hic I can get a Suburbs of
Chicago telephone phone book! I am in New <u>York!</u>"

"Lady, in the name of mercy—"

"Your name is "<u>Mercer</u>"?" she bumbels
"Then why did you say it was—"

"Look, sister, either you give me your
cousin Leon's phone number <u>right now</u> or I--"

"Are you <u>threatening me</u>?" she freezes.

"No, no, no! Do not hang up! I appologize.
Please, lady, just tell me what is your cousin's
<u>number??!</u>"

"I have it right here" comes thru the rye
(or Scotch and Boorbon for all I can tell).

"I know you do!" I coo, like ice. "You had
it 6 minuets ago! What—is—"

"It is —oh, darn! Wait a jiff. Where are
my reading glasses?"

"Ke-<u>ripes!</u>" I groan "How should I know
where are your reading glasses?"

"Ah, I believe they are in the hictchen"
she hics.

I could of brained that lush, assuming she
has one, but only cry "So zoom into the kitchen!"

"Hold the phone" she gives me. "Do not go
away."

"Where can I go?" I protest. "My mitt is
practicly <u>paralyzed</u> to this phone!"

Leo, by now I am ready to bust an ulcer and I
think I will be at least 100 bucks in the red if this
cockamamy tomato goes on, but I am determined to go
through with my quest, that being my nature as you
know from old times—and in no less than another
$2.75 the kookerino from "Come Back, Little Sheba"
comes back on the line, saying (cross my heart and
hope to die) "He-1-lo-o. Are you still there?"

"Yes—I—am—still—here, I am all ears

hanging on to your every word. What—is—his—number?!"

The bubblehead resites "The number is 6-4-1-8848."

"Thank you, and good ni—"

Are you sure you got it?" asks Miss Lonely-hearts. "It is 6-4-1—"

"8-8-4-8," I finish "Good ni—"

"The Area Code is 707—" that zombie croons.

O, man! I hear my blood boiling in my head and am ready to choke that monster to death with my own 2 hands or worse as I wimper "What area code?! Leo Rosten lives in New York, whose Area Code is the same one as you and me are conversing on!"

"My cousin "Leon" does not live in New York!" that crazy canary confides, as cold as a cuccumber "He lives near the city of Eureka, which is near Oregon, about twelve miles from—"

Well, to make a long story shorter, Leo, the way I slam that phone down sets me back another $15.00, which is what it cost Flo to fix her favorite lamp I nocked over.

—So, I guess you can see what I have gone through, pal! Holy Moses, why are you not listed in the Phone Book like any other law-abident citizen? What are friends for anyway, if not during an Emergency??!!

Leo, I do not mind telling you my nerves are still like shredded wheat from all the flak I went thru last night.

And I never even got to talk to you about the problem Flo and me have encountered, which is what I tried to phone you about in the first place!!

Disgusted, your old buddy

Herman ("Herm") Klitcher

P.S. I have typed all this out my-self, as you no dout agree, on account of Miss Ruby Olansky (my "Secretary") is a fruit-cake. She thought Bill of Lading was a friend of mine in Wyoming. And the way she chews gum whilst I dictate makes you think you are at West Point during target practise. But where can a guy get a Cracker-Jack steno. these days without finding Bubbel-gum in the box???

P.P.S. What _is_ your phone number?

P.P.P.S. If you dont get this letter be sure and let me know!

LEO ROSTEN
President
<u>"Unlisted Numbers:</u>
<u>The Fifth Freedom"</u>
Box 1776
Valley Forge
Iowa

Jan. 22

Herman P. Klitcher
Cinderella Laminated Shims, Inc.
83 Wacker Drive
Chicago, Ill. 60612

Dear "Herm":

    I certainly <u>was</u> knocked for a loop to hear
from you after only 26 years. Of course I remember
you. What member of our class could forget "Hermie
the Klitch," about whom our grad book said:
        "Keep your eyes on this cowboy!
        A real hot Go-getter. Flies
        won't grow on our "Herm'!!"
Judging from your letterhead alone, Herm,
not a single fly has grown on you.
    I read your letter with fascination. One
doesn't get letters like that every day, you know,
even if you are Ann Landers. I don't mean that I
enjoyed the miseries you had to endure, Person-
to-Person; I mean I was spellbound by the events
you so vividly described. (I was also glad to learn
about your wife Flo. What are the names of your
other wives?)

Belinda Rosten, whoever that is, is not
my cousin. I am not her cousin, either. In fact,
I never even heard of her until I received your missive.

It is true that I have an Unlisted Phone
Number, Herm. And I must tell you, in all honesty,
that it pleases me to hear that the telephone company so zealously protects the precious privacy
which an Unlisted Number provides.

My unlistedness is not meant as an affront
to old friends. I simply do not know how else to
escape calls from enterprising salesmen of deodor-
izers, cemetery plots, or Volunteers for Muskie.
In fact, I did not ask that my number be removed from
the telephone directory until the day I received
a call asking me to contribute some autographed
"personal article of clothing, whether a tie,
lock of hair, or old pair of tennis shoes" to a
raffle that was being held by The Friends of Piccolo
Players Who Contract Asthma.

There is another important reason I have
an Unlisted Number, Herm. It is this: I do not want
my number listed.

Your old pal,

Leo

P.S. What are laminated shims?

— L. R.

P.P.S. What brand of gum does Miss Olansky chew?

P.P.P.S. How in the world did you get my <u>address</u>?

— L

Freud
and
Monty O.

HERMAN P. KLITCHER
210 Placebo Park
Euphoria, Ill. 60035

Feb. 3

Leo Rosten
Apt. 39-A
Vesuvius Towers
644 E. 68 St.
New York, N.Y. 10021

Dear Leo:

Boy, was it ever a thrill to get a hand-written epistle from you and in your own writing!! My wife "Flo" who you never had the pleasure of meeting got such a kick out of hearing from a famous Author who isn't too stuck-up to answer one of his old H.S. buddies that she told me I must reply at once! Which I am doing.

You sure have not lost your humorus talents —like making up funny addresses for your-self! My wife Flo says only a "pro" author could come up with gasser like that! (But I am puzzeld by your asking what are the names of my "other" wives? Do you think I have turned into a <u>Morman</u> or something?! My wife Flo is the 1 and only female I have ever married, before or since!!)

So, please, old buddy, cut the clowning

around in re your answer to this missive. As you can see, I am penning you from my private home, in this exclusive and expansive Suburb we live in, only 21 miles N.E. of Chicago, that didn't even exist in your time in these environs.

You ask how did I get your address? It took some sharp angeling on my part, I can tell you. Because after I could not get you on Long Distance in N.Y. Flo said "Who out of your whole class at Crane Tech would be most libel to have Leo Rosten's phone number?" (You have to give Flo credit for allways being on the ball!)

So I thought about it—and bingo! Up popped the name of "Elmo Meckler". Remember Elmo? We use to call him "4-eyes" on account of his wearing glasses all the time, even in the showers. So I called Elmo, who is a big-time Lawyer here now, but he was in Pasadena or Mexico or some other God-forsaking place defending some guilty client— and his snippy Secretary would not even divulge the simple information I requested, "I _have_ Mr. Rostens address but it is strictly confidencial" she blabbed "unless Mr. Meckler gives his O.K.!!"

Can you beat that?

After I told her what she could do to Santa Claus (ha, ha) I thought about our old class some more—and the name of "Shmeley" Botnick invaded the old bean! You remember "Shmeley" don't you? The red-head we all the time kidded about twiching his nose like he lived inside the Stock Yards and couldnt stand the smell. Well, "Shmeley" is now a big name in Glass and Mirrors here in Chi.—tho he did not know your where-abouts either. But he came up with a _nifty_ idea—which was to call "Ace" Pojarsky, who works on the _Sun-Times_ here, and him being a crack Reporter just ask him!

Which I did. And good old "Ace" did not
let me down. He did not know your address off his
hand, he said, but would look you up in <u>Whose Who</u>
and see if you are in that important work of Information. And in 3 <u>seconds</u> he says into the phone "Hot
spit! Yes he is!!" So he gave it to me.

That is how come I got your address to write
you at. Now lets get down to brass roots.

It is about Montague O. Nayfish. He lives
next door to Flo and I in the house we have lived
in 11 years come next Octob. Any you would be pretty
proud, Leo, seeing the type house I have worked
up to. It is Split-Level Monteray, allthough
some people claim it looks more like a Cape of Cod
abode. (But not one of them ever fails to admire
the way it was furnished from top to toe by "Flo"
who I hope you will soon have the pleasure of meeting.)

Well, to get back to Montague O. (or "Monty"
as we all call him). He is a nice guy, with lots of
class, who uses Eau-de-Colon costs 20 smacks a
bottle and has made a Sensation and a <u>pile</u> of dough
in Wigs—for both the male and female sexes, which
he makes both Real and Artificial types of. Monty
is breaking new grounds in his "Nayfish System
of Hair Weaving", in which he weaves a person's
own hair <u>right into that person's own scalp!</u> (He
has a cute slogan for that: "Here Today—Hair
Tomorrow".) I guess you can see that Monty O. is
not one of your run-off-the-mills Wiggos.

Well, Monty O. has a real "Thing" about—
guess what? "Psyco-Analysis"!! He believes in
that stuff like it is the Bible. You can't even
raise a <u>question</u> about "Psyco-Analysis" without
Montys jumping down our neck like a ton of bricks.

16

Like if we are crazy enough to ask if the Astronuts
really got to the Moon (or are they giving us all
a big snow-job by showing Science Movies on the
Tube?)

To hear Monty O. brag about them, the "head
shrinkers" are practicaly the last hope we have
for Civilization to continue in its present form.
Because without them (the "Shrinks") the U.S.
could fall apart before the next election!!(Monty
refused to vote in the last 2 ones.)

Thats all we have been hassling about
lately when our gang gets together in Euphoria.
Until Flo exclaimed "Why are we trying to act like
experts on these complex matters when Hermie here
has a school buddy who can probly answer Monty
O. 1-2-3?!"

You see what I mean, Leo, about Flo allways
being right on the ball? She is not the type who
rolls over and hollers "Hooray! Hooray!" for
the kind of hokum-pokus Monty O. slings around!!
The way his talk is full of junk like "Sublimation"
"Edipuss Complex" "Aggression" or "Ambivulance"
is enough to drive a person crazy—if you are not
already there. If you know what I mean.

How in the name of carnation some people
go through life without their getting locked up
in what we used to call the Booby Hatch but now has
to be dolled up as a "Mental Institute"—well,
pal, it sure beats me!!! (Frankly, I think Monty
O. has been going to a Shrink his self for some time!)

So this is the purport of this letter—
Can you send us some snappy answers to the type
questions Monty (and his fellow Psycos, of who there
are quite a few) bat around? I mean real meat-and-
potatoe stuff—as follows:

17

1) What did Siegfried Freud actualy contribute to our stock of knowledge (about the cuckoo
behavior and ailiments of our fellow human
beings?)

2) Do you yourself think "Psyco-Analysis"
has cured people of anything—like stuttering,
hang-ups about Sex, fear of Super-Markets, and
etc.—all of which Monty himself had (but now says
he was totaly cured of, tho he wont tell by who!!)

3) Wouldnt Monty have gotten cured anyway
by useing plain common sense—without any Psyco-
Analysts?!

4) Why do their customers have to lay down
on a couch?

5) Why does the "Shrink" hide behind that
same couch?

6) Are dreams and feeling guilty and Sex
"perversion" all that important?!

Leo, I dont mind telling you I never had
a bad dream in my entire life. And I dont feel any
guilt about any thing! And I never had any type
Sex problem what-so-ever. (You can even ask Flo,
who certainly ought to know—ha!ha!—and she will
back me up 100% if shes a day.)

7) Finally, we keep getting our <u>ears</u> beat
off by the Nayfish crowds yakking about "Nurotics"
and "Psycotics." That lingo dont mean a thing
to me, and it cant pull the wool over Flos or my
2 eyes, but that is just what Monty tries to do with
them fancy un-American words!

So please dash off your explanations of
what these names actualy amount to, in a laymans
understanding. How do you yourself tell the diff??
Dont fail to overlook this important point.

Well, that about raps it up. Now it's up

to you, Leo—and I know you will hit the bulls-eye
with each answer!

Your friend,

Herman ("Herm") Glitcher

P.S. Me and Flo (my wife, ha, ha) feel lucky to pos-
sess a man like you among our circle of friends.

P.P.S. I do not comprehend why you want to know
what brand of gum Miss Ruby Olansky chews?? Thats
of no importance what-so-ever! Especially since I
have had to fire that taffy-head and have a whole
new Sec.—Miss Ileana Farfadetto, who is of Italian
dissent. She is a real "looker" and with a voice
like hot chocolat. Also she is very neat, but needs
plenty of braking-in. I think her English is shakey.
Her first day on the job I learn she thinks an "In-
voice" is what a singer should be on the day of a
concert.
            Man, the type help you have to put up with
these days!!

"H"

P.P.S. You mean to say an educated type intellect
like you dont even know about laminated shims??!
They are a very hot item—on a par with toggel-bolts
in home-building. Or zippers in mens pants.

LEO ROSTEN
Modish Coiffures and Head Shrinking
94 Ambivalent Blvd.
Palmistry Beach
Florida

February 11

Herman P. Klitcher
210 Placebo Park
Euphoria, Illinois

Dear "Herm":

Gosh, you certainly lead a rich, full life
in that exclusive, expansive Suburb only 21 miles
north-east of Chicago. (Is Euphoria near Wilmette,
or Grievance?)

Your friend Monty O. Nayfish is the kind of
hair-weaver I certainly would go to if I wanted
my own hair woven into my own scalp. But work of
that kind is so nerve-wracking, Herm, that I am
not surprised to hear that Monty has developed a
"thing" about Psychoanalysis. I would, too, if
I had to deal with the kind of clients who go to a
"Here Today Hair Tomorrow" salon.

Now, to get to your questions:

There can be no doubt that Siegfried Freud
contributed a great deal to psychology, while his
brother, Sigmund, was wasting his time living it
up with the Jet Set on the Italian Libido. For instance: Siegfried discovered the symbolic meaning
of the zipper (envy on the part of men trying to

close out that part of their problems). Siegfried also perfected a cure for spelling-bees. But it was Sigmund who exposed the imaginary origin of hallucinations, and the symbolic aspects of nail-clipping.

Psychoanalysis has been used with great success from pole to pole, Herm (although it has not been popular with other nationalities). The English, for example, will not even discuss their flower beds with anyone in the medical profession. (I doubt that any form of psychiatry can cure the average English woman's fixation on broccoli.)

The Swiss, for their part, don't pay much attention to Freud because they engage in sex only on Saturday nights during the "r" months. Switzerland has been independent for 300 years.

The French, of course, sneer at the mere mention of psychoanalysis, because by the time he is eight any French schoolboy knows how to add, subtract and multiply.

As for the Germans, Herm, their ideas about Sex are very orderly: They never indulge in it in front of their household pets, who get nervous during a copulation explosion.

I don't know about the Chinese, who are an inscrutable people; or the Japanese, who shout "Banzai!" whenever they get excited. That sort of thing would complicate anyone's sex life. Every time a Japanese man shouts "Banzai!" his partner thinks the Emperor is approaching. This means that a good deal of sex in Japan takes place while the women are bowing.

You ask, "Why do psychoanalytic patients lie on couches?" (That is not the only time they lie, of course.) You must remember that analysts' offices are often located in their homes, for tax purposes. And since analysts live in high-rent neighborhoods, many patients get so pooped trying to park their cars that they come down with Parkinson's Disease. But that is a problem for a Meter Maid, not a doctor.

I think you will agree, Herm, that if you want to stretch out, a couch is a lot more comfortable than a floor. And the first thing any good therapist wants is to make a patient comfortable. (The second thing he wants is to be comfortable himself: but he can't lie down; I doubt if anyone can do tip-top therapy from a hard floor 8-10 hours a day.)

But, Herm, no analyst actually "hides" behind the patient's couch. Analysts <u>lurk</u> behind the couch, say in a chair that tilts back like a barber's chair. In this position a psychoanalyst is better situated to pursue his own free-associations. What the whole psychoanalytic process boils down to is a mental ping-pong match between the free-associations of patient and doctor. The former free-associates out loud, but the latter free-associates in silence—so as not to confuse the former.

I was especially interested in your saying that you have never felt guilty. Herm, you should not feel guilty about not feeling guilty.

As for your statement that you have never had any Sex problems whatsoever—keep up the good work, Herm!! I am sure Flo will agree with this.

Now, for the tough part of your letter: the difference between Neurotics and Psychotics. First, they are spelled differently. This is important, Herm—especially if you are either. Neurotics get extremely upset by incorrect spelling, and psychotics think you are persecuting them by using a secret vocabulary.

I know of a case where an Intern at one of our finest hospitals wrote ".Lo" after "Blood Pressure" on the admission form for a patient who staggered into the Emergency ward. The Intern happened to be thinking about the pressure in his bicycle tires, but how could the attending M.D. know that? Herm, they had that poor patient doing so many knee-bends and push-ups that by the time the Intern's tires contained normal pressure, the patient had grown such knots in his varicose veins that they had to replace 3 yards of them with nylon. This is just an example.

You ask how do I distinguish between Neurotics and Psychotics? That is easy:

A psychotic is an out-and-out loon. He may think his father is poisoning his yoghurt, that his wife is planning to strangle him with noodles, or that the U.S. Government should flood Las Vegas with soda water. A neurotic, on the other hand, is a determined sufferer, afflicted by things like depressed cuticles, a fear of pistachio nuts, or underarm humidity.

To put it most simply, a psychotic thinks 2 plus 2 equals 7 (4 is the correct answer). A neurotic knows that 2 plus 2 equals 4—but he just can't stand it.

Here are some simple tests you can use, even in Euphoria, to tell the difference between neurotics and psychotics—and I'll bet Monty O. will turn green with envy when you try these out before his eyes on any member of your gang:

1) Salutation Test

When you say "Hello" to a neurotic, he is likely to bridle, "What do you mean by that?" When you say "Hello" to a psychotic, he will go to the bathroom.

2) Rorschach Test

Show two subjects, male or female (or both), an ink-blot such as this:

The subject who says "That is a goddam ink-blot!" is neurotic. The one who exclaims "That is a Rorschach Test, designed to trap me into revealing my childhood fantasies about my mother's reticule!" is on the right track.

3) Dream Interpretation

A neurotic is happy to elaborate on his dreams for hours. He will even project them for you, along with color slides of his trip to "Nature's Winter Wonderland."

A psychotic, on the other hand, confuses dreams with reality, and he will accuse you of stealing his dreams—and run away. Don't let this worry you, Herm. As Freud taught us, a psychotic is least dangerous when egos away.

4) Direct Interrogation

I happen to think that the best way to find out whether someone is neurotic or psychotic is by asking him. Seat the subject in an easy chair and, in a casual tone of voice, smile, "By the way, John, would you describe yourself as being alive?"

If the answer is "Yes," that rules out psychosis. If the answer is "No," do not jump to conclusions until you have listened to the subject's heart with a stethoscope. (Of course, you should never address a subject as "John" if his name is Sam, Percy, or Beulah. You can ruin the

Direct Interrogation test by addressing a subject in a way that arouses his suspicions.)

Well, that about wraps it up, Herm. I hope I hit those bulls right in the eye.

Your buddy,

Leo

P.S. What are laminated shims?

**From the Desk of
Herman P. Klitcher**

Feb. 19

Dear Leo:

In re your long epistle of the 11th—<u>Were
you kidding, or giving us the inside lowdown??</u>

"Herm"

Feb. 25

Dear Desk of Herman Klitcher:

Yes.

—Desk of Leo Rosten

P.S. I have re-read "Cinderella" but find no
reference (however esoteric) to "laminated shims."

From the Desk of
Herman P. Klitcher

Feb. 28

Dear Leo:

  Very funny (ha) to reply "Dear Desk"—
but still you duck my question! Do not think I did
not notice.

  But I am not the type who has a "thin skin"
so I say no more and will not even ignore it.

  I am surprised an educated man like you
doesnt know what are laminated shims!! If you will
meerly turn your mind back to our Wood Shop class
at Crane where we had Mr. Steuben (that holy terrier
who made us plane a board to 90°—so no light past
under the "square" we had to move down the whole
edge of that board, like we were making a bookshelf
for the King of Rumania). Remember those thin
"wedges" we used to use, to prop up under a door
before making hinges to keep it (the door) level?

  Well, buster, in case you did not know it,
those were Shims! And "laminated" means they are
made in layers welded together for strenth—a
real hot item in these times of homebuilding &
other construction.

    Your buddy of old,

     "Herm"

P.S. The story of "Cinderella" has got nothing
to do with it! That is just the name that Flos Old
Man, who is the founder and Pres. of the Company,
chose as the name of the company! He loves the story.

"H"

P.P.S. What is "esoteric"?

Mar. 1

Dear Desk:

So that's what "shims" are! I thought they
had something to do with the dance Joan Crawford
made popular.

"Esoteric" is the name of a tooth-paste,
made from herbs on the island of Esot, just outside
Death Valley.

Leo

P.S. What is Flo's father's favorite book after
"Cinderella"?

**From the Desk of
Herman P. Klitcher**

Mar. 5

Dear Leo—

Our son Alvin and "Penny" (our oldest
daughter) are real whizzers in Geog. and they say
there is <u>no island of any type</u> near or just outside
Death Valley. That is strictly desert country!!

"*Herm*"

P.S. Flos old man is not a big reader.

How to Tell
Your Child
About S-E-X-

Cinderella LAMINATED SHIMS
83 Wacker Drive
Chicago, Illinois 60612

Mar. 9

Leo Rosten
Apt. 39-A
Vesuvius Towers
644 E. 68 St.
New York, N.Y. 10021

Dear Leo:

To be absolutley frank and above the boards
about it, Leo, me and my wife Flo read your epistle
about Psyco-analysis over maybe 9 times before
Flo surmised that you must of been "pulling our
legs"! I told Flo you are not the type who goofs
off with an old pal, but she says there is no other
way to interperet your remarks in re sex among the
Swiss, Japs, and etc.

Speaking of that subject (Sex) inspires
me to get your advice about something. A big argument
bust out at a party at "Frenchy" Lastfogel's
abode last Sat.—on the subject of what is the best
way to answer a kid when he or she asks you "Where
do babies come from?"

Leo, the ideas some of those friends ex-
pressed on this subject were just <u>disgusting</u>!
Some of the marrieds went "all out" for telling
a child the blunt and naked "Facts of Life"—

which goes against my grains. Other persons present
opined that you have to "dress up" the ugly facts
on account they can so mix up a sensitive kid that
he or she will be a sitting duck for a head-shrinker
by the time they hit 21.

Like for instance, our son Alvin. He is 16
going on 17 at the present time. Well, Alvin has
begun to drop hints to his Mother and I about The
Subject—and says he wants to get the dope "right
from the horses mouth." That means me, natch—
although I am not a horse, and Flo says that the
way I drink on festive occassions I have a mouth
more like a fish, ha, ha!

Anyway, after the party at "Blitz" and
"Frenchys" (he is called "Blitz" on account
he is a killer at gin Rummy) was concluded, Flo
and me are in the private aroma of our bed-room,
talking things over. And we decide "Before we
maybe damage Alvin's entire future outlook on
girls (or even on boys, the way things are these
days) should we consult Oswald Spitzer, our Doctor,
who is a jerk—or should we read up on the best modern
straight-from-the-sholder books about Sex?"

Then Flo has a real inspiration! Exclaiming
"Hey, dummy, why do we not ask your old friend
Leo?!! He no dout got through God-knows-how-many-
colleges so he probly knows the best answer to this
question in all its pluses and minuses as far as
the child is concerned!"

So heres our question, Alfred Einstein:
"How is the best way to answer your kid when he
comes right out and asks you "Where do babies
come from"?"!

I hope you will be absolutely open and frank
about this, Leo, and not give us that old jazz about
the Birds and the Bees. We already told Alvin about

the Birds and the Bees, but he said he cant understand how his own Mother laid eggs, and asks me
"Where do you get your pollen from, Dad?" !X#&%!

        Or should we put the whole blame on the
Stork? (That is pretty hard to put over on a kid
with a base voice going on 17!)

        Please answer fast, Leo, because from 1
or 2 little things I have observed lately, Alvin
is in a hurry! (I even think he is using Afrodisiacs,
from the type of pictures of naked broads he has
slapped all over his room.) And so is your old pal,

Herman ("Herm") Klitcher

P.S. What is your private home phone number?

LEO ROSTEN
<u>Sex Counsellor</u>
606 Wassermann Drive
Cocksackie, N.Y., 10051

March 14

Herman Klitcher
Cinderella Laminated Shims, Inc.
83 Wacker Drive
Chicago, Ill. 60612

Dear "Herm":

To get right to the question that is bothering you and your wife, Flo: "What is the best way
to tell your kid about where babies come from?"
Herm, that question has plagued mankind
down the centuries. Last year alone, 9.7% of the
Federal budget was spent on research by psychiatrists for the U.S. Navy who are studying the least
harmful way of telling American sailors "the
facts of life," in case they are ship-wrecked,
find themselves on a desert island, meet beautiful
native girls and don't know where to begin.
You have no idea how many nice American
boys are confused about the very question that
is bothering your son Alvin. (By the way, what are
the names of your other sons?)
I happen to know <u>exactly</u> how one should
answer a child who asks: "Where do babies come
from?" There are 3 simple rules to keep in mind,
Herm:

1) Do not hit him.

2) Tell the absolute truth.

3) Since the truth is probably as upsetting to you and Flo as to Alvin, dress the facts up in the suit that best fits your child's psychological shape.

Let me illustrate by telling you how I told "the facts of life" to my own children.

Case 1

My son, Philo. Philo was a gentle, sensitive lad, who was very popular with insects. He was constantly being bitten by horseflies, hornets, yellow-jackets and bees. I think you will agree, Herm, that in his case it would have been <u>disastrous</u> to mention "the birds and bees," because he might have ended up thinking that if you bite a girl, the way he did all through nursery school, you make her pregnant.

How well I remember the day Philo first asked me about Sex. It was a Tuesday. "Dad," he blurted, "where do babies come from?"

At once I replied. "Son, how old are you?"

He counted on his fingers. "Twenty-three."

"Twenty-<u>three!</u>" I echoed. "My, my, where does the time go? It seems like only yesterday you were twenty-two."

"Yesterday I <u>was</u> twenty-two," said Philo. "Today is my birthday."

"Happy birthday, son," I smiled.

"Quit stalling, Pater," he sneered. "<u>Where did I come from?</u>"

Well, Herm, at that point I could not fake a heart attack, as I had been planning to do for years, so I sighed, "Okay, Philo. Sit down. I have something important to tell you."

When he was comfortably seated on his cat, I told him the simple truth: that he had been left on our doorstep by someone I certainly would like to get my hands on.

Herm, I have never regretted my candor.

<u>Case 2</u>

My daughter, Madrilene. Madrilene was a sweet, average American girl with an inordinate number of teeth in need of straightening because our dentist was building a ballroom over his garage.

One day, right out of the blue, Madrilene asked me, "Dadsy, where does a baby come from?"

Without a moment's hesitation, I answered, "Whose baby?"

"Any baby," she replied.

"<u>Any</u> baby?" I retorted. "That's a pretty sloppy way to ask a question! Just suppose I talked that way, Maddy. Suppose I asked you: 'Where do Popsicles come from?' You'd answer 'Which Popsicle?' wouldn't you?"

"I would not," said Madrilene, "since the only place in this crummy town that sells Popsicles is Schermerhorn's."

"That's true," I said, studying my palms. "Now be a good girl and go play with your Lucrezia Borgia doll."

"I don't have a Lucrezia Borgia doll," said Madrilene.

"Goodness," I chuckled. "Did you lose her?"

"No, I set fire to her. Stop stalling, Dads: Where—do—babies—come—from?"

"Very well," I said firmly. I took a deep breath and declaimed, "I happen to have made a careful study of Doctors Spock, Rock, Gesell,

Ilg and every pamphlet on this subject published
by the Child Study Association. The simple truth,
dear, is—I just don't believe their version of
how it is done! Don't get me wrong, darling. I know
where babies come from (and so do you, judging from
the wicked little grin on your puss). What I don't
understand, frankly, is how they get there."

Herm, I have never had reason to regret my
frankness.

Case 3

My third child, Peggotty. Peg was always
an innocent, trusting child who majored in dangling
participles. She was busy finger-painting the
wallpaper in her room, one night, when I came in
looking for my pipe cleaners. (I always had to
scour my kids' rooms to find a pipe cleaner, Herm,
because the three of them got straight A's in "Creative Uses of Pipe Cleaners," a course in which they
learned the most ingenious adaptations of pipe
cleaners to purposes other than the cleaning of
pipes: making epileptic skeletons, extremely thin
dinosaurs, removing bubble-gum from our pancake
syrup, cleaning the blood off their scalping knives,
etc.)

Well, the minute I walked into Peggotty's
room, Herm, I was greeted by this question: "Okay,
Pop, let's have it: What about Sex?"

At once, in the most frank, forthright
tone, I replied, "What do you mean, 'What about
Sex'?"

"You know perfectly well what I mean!"
humphed Peggotty.

"That is true," I sighed.

"Well?"

"Well what?"

"What—about—Sex?"

Herm, I was right up against the moment
every American father dreads. But I knew exactly
what to say. After all, I had gone through this
identical crisis twice before and had learned a
thing or two. So I took my little girl's hands into
my own and gently said: "Listen carefully, Peg,
because I don't want you ever to believe the silly,
nasty things you may hear from other children. I
want to talk to you like a modern father talking
to an intelligent, modern child."

"I'll be late for my karate class," she
whined.

"I'll come right to the point," I assured
her. "Now, take a rose. It smells. It smells <u>nice,</u>
right? Well, it just so happens that <u>that same</u>
<u>smell happens to smell nice to a honeybee, too!</u>
So when a Papa Bee gathers nectar from the rose, he
picks up pollen on his back legs, which he rubs off
on a female rose or a Mama Bee—"

"Oh, <u>God,</u>" Peggotty moaned. "When I
asked you 'What about Sex?' all I meant is what do
I write in <u>here?</u>" And she held before my eyes a
printed form:

NAME: <u>Peggotty Rosten</u>

DATE OF BIRTH: <u>July 4, 1957</u>

SEX: _____

"What," I asked, "is this?"
"My application for college," said Peg.
"Write in 'F!'" I said firmly, "That
stands for 'Female.' By George, Peggotty, you are
old enough to know: You—are a girl!"

Herm, I have never regretted my candor.

Your old pal,

Leo

P.S. % #!&!!

Cinderella LAMINATED SHIMS
83 Wacker Drive
Chicago, Illinois 60612

March 18

Leo Rosten
Apt. 39-A
Vesuvius Towers
644 E. 68 St.
New York, N.Y. 10021

Dear Leo—

Ce-ripes, there you go again! Winging it,
like a real Psyco in your type answering. What
else can I (or Flo, who agrees) even say in inter-
pereting such cockamamy examples about Sex as you
wrote? We even dout those 3 peculier "children"
you say you have! We bet you just made them up!

Your old pal,

"Herm"

P.S. Even my son Alvin agrees—and he is no nuckel-
head!

LEO ROSTEN
Expert on Appositives
Punctuation,
North Dakota

Mar. 21

Herman P. Klitcher
210 Placebo Park
Euphoria, Illinois

Dear Herm:

What are the names of your other sons?

Yours,

Leo

**From the Desk of
Herman P. Klitcher**

Dear Leo—

Man, you are really something!! I inform you
I have only one wife Flo and you come back and ask for
the names of our "other" sons—when we dont have
more than the 1 in question (Alvin)!!

Are you sure you are feeling O.K.? You sound
like you are on a marry-go-around.

To prevent future mis-understandings on
your part, pal, I will give you the whole Klitcher
line-up—

1) Alvin (son) 17

2) Penelope ("Bubbles") 16

3) Mildred, 15 (who everyone calls "Pidge"
on account of her love for those animals, which she
raises and keeps in a coot on top of our garage)

4) Hortense (our final, who we call "Baby") age 12.

That is the <u>whole</u> kid-and-caboodle of the
Klitcher family!

I will go even farther. Alvin was named
after Flos grandfather (Alvin S. Krumbach, who
lived to be 82 and saw a good deal of Alvin). "Penelope" was a made-up name that me and Flo liked because of its nick-name possibility—"Penny".
(So instead everyone called her "Bubbles" on
account of her personality even whilst an infant.)
Mildred was named in honor of my Aunt Mildred, may
she rest in peace (in the cemetery in Chi. where she

lays.) And Hortense ("Baby") bares her name after
Flos Aunt—who past away 2 years ago right after our
Thanksgiving family get-together. (Dr. Debris says
it was "cardiac arrest" due to over-eating greasey
foods, but I happen to know he is jealous of Flos
cooking, which is 1000% better than his wife ever
turns out! If you took a secret vote, Mrs Debris
would win it hands down as the worst cook in Euphoria! Which is saying a mouth-full.)

I hope this answers all your unexplaned
questions in the future!

Your old buddy,

"Herm"

P.S. What is your home phone?

LEO ROSTEN
Family Recorder
74 Heritage Drive
Ancestry
Alabama

Mar. 26

Herman P. Klitcher
210 Placebo Park
Euphoria, Illinois 60035

Dear Herm:

My home phone is a white, "cradle" model, with a dial, manufactured by Western Electric for the Bell Telephone System, a subdivision of A.T. and T.

Your friend,

Alexander Graham

**From the Desk of
Herman P. Klitcher**

Dear Leo—

     For G---sake! Do you <u>allways</u> have to clown around? <u>Pretending</u> you mistake the plain meaning of a simple question?! Like: "Whats your home phones number"??

                  Disgusted,

                    "Herm"

Dear "Disgusted":

I'm sorry for all these misunderstandings.
They only go to show how hard it is for two grown boys
to communicate.

My home phone's number is Mod. 2-OD-469- C/ M
33-PATENTED.

Yours,

Leo

**From the Desk of
Herman P. Klitcher**

Dear Leo—

    Cant you get off your yo-yo?? I will not
even <u>comment</u> on your giving me the Serial No. of your
telephone, which does me no good what-so-ever as far
as calling you is conserned.

    This is too "far out" jokery for me and my
wife Flo as well. So the shoe is on the others foot,
Mac!!

    Have you been sick lateley? Or have you lost
many marbels thru meer ageing?

               Your chum,

                 "*Herm*"

From the
Desk
of
Leo Rosten

April 1

Dear Desk of Herman Klitcher:

Since reading your fascinating epistles, I
have aged considerably.

Yours,
Desk of

Leo Rosten

The Great
"That/Which"
Debate

PENELOPE KLITCHER

April 7

Dear Mr. R—

My folks say it is O.K. to write you for help about a problem in English.

Well, I could just spit I am so T'd off! At Miss Raskolnikov. Our English teacher. She has shot me down. On an exam. She said my way of employing "that" and "which" shows I do not even begin to understand the diff. between them!

Well, WHO DOES? Her explaining did not do any of us any good at ALL! Every one in the class is mixed-up.

You are the only person I can think of who maybe <u>does</u> know when to employ "that" and likewise "which". Are you?

Please give examples.

Thanking you for your real help and aid to a deserving student,

Your Friend
(who hates being called
"Bubbles" which everyone does)

Penelope ("Penny")

April 11

Dear "Penny":

    Not knowing the correct way to use "that"
and "which" is nothing to be ashamed of. Neither
is ending a sentence with a preposition.

    Grammarians have gone dippy trying to ex-
plain when to use "that" and when to use "which."
Some authorities committed suicide after other authorities found scandalous errors in their (the first
authorities') explanations of "that which"ing.

    I happen never to have found this a problem.
The rules I follow are so simple, Penny, that I am
confident they will end your worries forever:

    1) Use "who" when referring to the offi-
cials of an underdeveloped country.

    2) Use "that" in discussing "which."

    3) Use "which" for all articles made of
rubber.

    4) Never use "who" for animals, except
owls.

    5) The only time to use "<u>that</u> which" is
when discussing the historic trials in Salem, Mass.

    Perhaps the best way to illustrate these
subtleties, Penny, is to send you a copy of the letter I wrote Immanuel Kant, after the appearance of
his trail-blazing <u>Lapsed Conjunctions</u>:

    Dear Manny:

        That that "that" is different

from this "that" is as obvious as that
this "this" is different from that
"this," this "that," that "that,"
or those "thems."

     <u>All</u> of these, may I remind you, are
examples of proper usage in cases where a
"that" is called for and a "which" is
not.

                           Yours,

                        Leo

     If you will memorize this letter, "Penny,"
you will be the envy of all your classmates.

                       Your friend,

                    Mr. R—

P.S. Is Miss Raskolnikov related to the Feodor Dostoevskis?

HERMAN P. KLITCHER
210 Placebo Park
Euphoria, Ill. 60035

Leo Rosten
Apt. 39-A
Vesuvius Towers
644 E. 68 St.
New York, N.Y. 10021

Dear Leo—

Me and Flo have practicly broken our <u>necks</u>
trying to find out if there are any "Doestoevskis"
in our neck of the woods (after our "Penny" showed
us your wonderfull letter about good English).
There is not 1 single name like that in the Chicago
Suburban Telephone book. And no one we asked (here in
Euphoria or any nearby town, including Skokie) ever
even heard of any family or human called "Dostoevski!"

Leo, <u>are you sure you spelled that name</u>
<u>right?!</u> It could be Hungarian or Albanian, you know.
Those aliens allways changed their names spelling
when they hit the good old U.S.A.—especialy when
that name ended in "ski."

So if you can give us more dope maybe we will
find a family who they <u>originaly</u> bore the name of
"Dostoevski."

Me and Flo sure would like to help you out

after all the time and sweat you have put in so far
for all of us!!

Your buddy,

"Herm"

P.S. What makes you think Miss Raskolnikov is con-
nected with the family in question?

LEO ROSTEN
Professor of Slavic
1064 Karenina Place
Vitebsk
U.S.S.R.
Zip Code: ГЯФЕ

Herman P. Klitcher
210 Placebo Park
Euphoria, Illinois

Dear "Herm"—

    Ask Miss Raskolnikov.

                    Yours,

                    Leo

The
Secret Shame of
Miss Raskolnikov

Mrs. Herman P. Klitcher
201 Placebo Park
Euphoria, Ill. 60035

April 19

Leo Rosten
Apt. 39-A
Vesuvius Towers
644 E. 68 St.
New York, N.Y. 10021

Dear <u>Cher Ami</u> Leo:

I hope you do not mind my getting into this
exchange of <u>billets</u> and calling you "Leo" instead
of "Mister Rosten," when the only reason I even
<u>know</u> you is because of your being an ex-classmate of
my hubby 2 score and 20 years ago, as A. Lincoln said.
But from everything Hermie has told me about you—
and from perusing your <u>marvy</u> letters (even when they
are in jest, and evading our questions, a man as busy
as you is very <u>gentil</u> to answer at all)—I feel I
know you like a book, having read many of them ever
since I was a maiden, including more than one of yours!
Anyway, here goes, Leo—and please do not
be bashful about calling me "Flo", instead of
"Florence" or "Florrie", which is what the
girls at our local Seeds and Shrubs Society call me.
(<u>Entre nous,</u> I <u>hate</u> "Flossie"—which is what my

dentist calls me. His name is "Lipschitz"—but I
do not call him "Lip"!)

To get right to the point of this petit
memoire (as you can see, I j'adore French, having
taken 4 corses in that beautiful language, and I
know you must be a cannoiseur of it).

Your hint to my hubby about us asking Miss
Raskolnikov herself (if she is in any way related to
the "Dostoevskis") was the perfect smart thing to
do! So I had a little tete-a-tete talk with Miss R.
(after school last Wednesday, the 16th)—and the
whole problem has been cleared up to I hope your satisfaction as well as our's!

Miss Frieda Raskolnikov is not related to
the Dostoevskis. She informed me herself. She says
you have mixed up a famous Russian author (Theodore
Dostoevski) with a character or relative, which
she is not. This famous author wrote many novels—of
which the most popular of all of them is called
"Crimes of Punishment" (in its English transla-
tion). And the main character in that master-piece
(according to Miss R.) was named "Raskolnikov."

But he was a murderer, so our Miss Raskolnikov does not like to be considered a possible relative of his in any shape, manner or form!! And I do
not blame her.

Miss R. went on to confide to me that her
family did originally come from the Caucus Mountain
neighborhood, and they were called "Raskolnikov-
ski"—but her grand-father chopped the "ski"
off of that nom de famille in 1894, to make it less
of an alien name and more in the Anglo-Saxon line—
which is just what you suspected in your letter to
Herm!

We certainly have to hand it to you for
detective work, Leo! All of us in the Klitcher house-

hold have been discussing this whole interesting
aspect of Immigration to the U.S.
    <u>Merci</u> loads,

                                    Your friend,

                                      "Flo"

P.S. Do you have any ideas of what the name "Klitcher" might have been in "the old country"? Don't
let on to Hermie that I asked!

LEO ROSTEN
President
Ethnic Derivations, Inc.
United Nations Plaza
Geneva,
Spain

April 27

Mrs. Herman P. Klitcher
210 Placebo Park
Euphoria, Illinois, 60035

Chère "Flo"—

    I was wondering when I would hear directly
from you, after the brouhaha in which I have become
involved with other members of your charming family.
    They can tar and feather me before I so much
as drop a hint to Herm (or anyone else) that you asked
me to delve into the origins of "Klitcher."
    One would think, at first glance, that
"Klitcher" is of German or Persian origin. But
careful research proves this not to be the case.
There was a family called "Klister" in Klosters,
up to the 19th Century, but they were all wiped out in
an avalanche (1895). And there was a family called
"Clintzer" in the Zuyder Zee, around the time of
Napoleon, but they drowned when the dikes col-
lapsed (1816).
    Flo, I can find no language which contains
"Klitcher" as either a word or name—except, just
possibly, a dialect spoken in Bechuanaland, where

"Klikklich" refers to a small animal, not unlike a
kinkajou, which lives in trees and prowls about only
at night.

I see no reason to assume that this has the
slightest bearing on Hermie.

Your _ami_,

Leo

P.S. There is a Tchambouli tongue in which "Chich-
er" refers to wrestlers who come down with the
croup; but from what I remember about your _mari_ he
never was much of a wrestler.

Mrs. Herman P. Klitcher
201 Placebo Park
Euphoria, Ill. 60035

April 30

Leo Rosten
Apt. 39-A
Vesuvius Towers
644 E. 68 St.
New York, N.Y. 10021

<u>Cher ami</u> Leo:

What a fascinating letter! Your store-
house of knowledge about various things is certainly
an amazing sight to behold! (To say nothing of the
addresses you dream up, which are a riot!)
While chatting with him the other night
(Thursday) I <u>casually</u> asked Hermie if he had ever
been a wrestler—or come down with the croup. His
answers make me think you are right, as usual. So
you do not have to <u>exploréz</u> the problem of family
names any further. Because (said Hermie) his only
youthfull wrestling was on "dates" in the back
seat of the cars of that vintage. As I was one of the
"dates" he had, I do not hold this against him.
For I am the <u>femme</u> he <u>cherchezed</u>!
As to the "croup," the closest he ever

came to having any chest or lung ailments was when
he was 10 years of age and came down with chicken-
pox.

       <u>Merci beaucoups</u> anyways, Leo, for trying.

                Your friend

                   "*Flo*"

P.S. I never <u>dreamed</u> any of the fellows at Crane
Tech even bothered to absorb such interesting,
off-the-beat information as you display about the
Dutch and other primitive tribes.

                        —F.

P.P.S. I am <u>très</u> glad you did not connect Klitcher
to Raskolnikov!

The Truth
about the
Humboldt Current

ALVIN P. KLITCHER

May 2

Dear Mr. L. Rosten—

Excuse me for writing you, but it was my
old man's idea—so blame him.

I am beating my brains out for our exam
in Geog. which it is always a ball-buster. Our
teacher is Mr. J. Bulbemann, a real monster with
no mercy for students.

I know he will ask about things like where
is some creepy country in Nigeria or some other
area no one except him ever heard of. Another sneak
thing he likes to pull is a <u>trick question</u>—like
describe "the Hummbold Current."

Well, he hardly even <u>mentioned</u> that in class
except the once when he tossed it off like it was
poison. That is why he likes to spring it as a foxy
question. That is the type of teacher he is!

I asked my old man about it (the Hummbold
Current) but he was no help at all, saying, "I do
not clutter up my brain-pan with cockamamy stuf
like that."

"Well, can I ask Mr. Leo Rosten, who
does?" I asked him.

"That's a nifty idea," he said. "He
probly can give you the dope, if he levels with you
and does not horse around, as he is prone to with
members of our family."

So please do not horse around Mr. R.

For this up-coming quiz, I have memmorized
the heighths of Mt. Everett and the difference between Latitudes and Longitudes that line up from
Greenwich England, and even iron production around
Gary, Minn. But I am just a blank in a deep-freez
about the Hummbold Current! I have looked it up in
two reference books without any luck even finding
it.

Can you help me out?

Awaiting your expert help with real thanks,

Your friend Herman Klitcher's son,

Alvin ("Al")

P.S. I do not need a long answer. Just the brute
facts.

LEO ROSTEN
President
Oceanic Consultant Association
Atlantis
Peru

May 6

Dear "Al":

You do not need luck to find the Humboldt
Current; you need to know how to spell it. Two "m"s
and no "t" are what led you on a wild goose chase,
and if there is any current which wild geese despise
it is Humboldt's.

If you just memorize the brutal facts,
Alvin, Mr. J. Bulbemann will be astounded.

1) The Humboldt Current is in the Pacific
Ocean. It is the brother-in-law of the Andreas
Fault, which hangs around Santa Barbara.

2) The Humboldt Current is nowhere in or
near Humboldt County. (There are counties named
"Humboldt" in Iowa, Nevada and California.) Keep
that in mind, Alvin, because it is a favorite trick-
play Geography teachers have used for fifty years
to trip up a student.

3) The Humboldt Current is only another name
for the Peruvian Current. It contains cold water,
flowing northward off the coasts of Chile and Peru,
where I have a peanut grove.

4) The chilly temperature of the Peruvian
Current is what causes all the fogs, aridity and
cases of grippe in these areas. That is how Chile
got its name.

5) On January 6, 1971, the Humboldt Current burned to the ground. Further questions about it are academic.

Your father's friend,

Mr. L. Rosten

P.S. Don't stop with latitudes and longitudes, Al. Brush up on your isotherms.

from

ALVIN ("AL") KLITCHER

Dear Mr. R—

I am very gratefull to you (for your reply.)
Your dope turned out to be a <u>godsend</u>—even tho Mr.
Bulbemann never even asked us about the Hum<u>boldt</u>
Current! (or "isotherms".)

He asked us about Zones of Climate, the
Equator, and the 3 longest rivers in the world.
As I could only think of 2 longest rivers (the Nile
and the Volgo) I pulled a neat switcheroo on the
Monster by writing on my exam paper:

"Both these long rivers are outside the U.S.—but if you count rivers
that are <u>under water,</u> like <u>The Humboldt
Current,</u> then that one is long enough to
qualify." (Then I told the stuff you told
me about it—except its burning to the
ground. That would have <u>creamed</u> me with Mr.
B.—who has no cents of humor.)

My father was right. You are a real friend
in need!

Your friend's son,

Alvin ("al")

P.S. Am waiting to get the marked exam back. Any day now. I am pretty confident about my answers, but you never can tell about the Monster's.

Dear Alvin:

The Monster whom you tell me of
Is not the type you're meant to love;
Just now, his most essential feature
Is how he grades you, as your teacher.

                                    Mr. R—

ALVIN ("AL") P. KLITCHER

Dear Mr. R—

    The marks (for the Geog. exam) are in. With your help I got a C— on that unfair and lousé (as my mother would say) quiz. Still, I know I have to take the bad with the worst—which would be to flunk it cold!

    Mr. Bulbemann wrote a kind of wierdo remark on my paper:

       "Alvin—
Have you had your glasses checked recently? Your comments on the Humboldt Current are disturbing. They seem to combine fact with insanity in a way I have not encountered before.
       —J.B.
P.S. Perhaps you should get a general medical examination.

Mr. R—Can you <u>tie</u> that?!

             Your friend,

             "Al"

P.S. Mr. B. has stopped calling on me in class. In fact, the minute I come into Room 202 the Monster turns pale, or goes to open a window, even when it is cold outside. He has become very nervus lately.

LEO ROSTEN, M.D.
Tics and Neurology
Topeka Clinic
Vienna

May 12

Dear Alvin P. Klitcher:

The Humboldt Current has strange effects
upon hyper-sensitive teachers. So do I.

Yours truly,

Leo Rosten, M.D.

P.S. So do you, it seems. Follow Mr. Bulbemann's
advice; get a thorough medical examination. And
ask the doctor to keep a sharp eye out for what is
technically known as the Humboldt Syndrome. In this
rare but common psychological disorder, all the
bolts in the patient's system give off a faint hum-
ming sound. This is nothing to get alarmed about.
It merely means that the current in the patient's
body needs re-tuning.

— R. R.

P.P.S. In a recent case of Humboldt Syndrome I was
consulted on, the patient could not even get the
local weather report; within two days after therapy
began, he was enjoying high-frequency broadcasts
of Shani Krishna playing "Pale Hands I Loved Beside
the Shalimar" on the zither. From Calcutta.

—M.D.

The
Menace of
Ronald Blish

Mrs. Herman P. Klitcher
201 Placebo Park
Euphoria, Ill. 60035

May 15

Mr. Leo Rosten
Apt. 39-A
Vesuvius Towers
644 E. 68 St.
New York, N.Y. 10021

<u>Cher ami</u> Leo:

        Now that we have "broken the ice" I feel
as if I have a real new friend in who I can confide
some of my most <u>intime</u> (not "in time", but French)
thoughts and personal problems as they arise from
time to time. I feel you are very sympatico to the
burdens and heartakes of others!
        So I hope you will not think me pushy or
just trying to get the Autograph of a TV personality,
as we all know you to be, having seen you on the "Kup
Show" which we watch even tho it is coming on later
and later at night.
        <u>Alors!</u> We have run into a real problem in
the Klitcher household. This is something that
has caused Herm and I many a sleep-less night's
worrying! It is about our Penelope, who everyone

calls "Bubbles", which is her nature. Entre
nous, Leo, I think she is also spending many a sleep-
less night. Because she has a real "hang-up"
about a boy-friend by the name of Ronald Blish—who
in my opinion is giving her the whole "romantic"
bit, like Clark Gable gave Claudette Colburn in
"It Happened One Night." (Remember that oldie??
It is still one of my favorite pix. The way Clark
moved in on Claudette at the end, with that Bugle
over the blanket remains one of my favorite movie
memories of all time!)

Well, Bubble's B.F. phones our girl 10-20
times per day, and he dated her for the Shimmel
High School Boogaloo Dance—which did not conclude
until 1:30 in the morning, but that was 3 hours
before he got her home! And she came in looking
like she had been playing house (or worse) with
a Polar bear.

You see, this Ronald Blish has a Tokyo-type
car, his father being a Cement Contractor and loaded
(as Herm happened to check on). And he (Ronald)
uses that Jap car to drive Bubbles around—5-6
hours at a crack (not counting parking in certain
places) and gets her home way past the wee-wee
hours. God only knows what goes on in non-stop
smoochings of that duration (if you know what I
mean.) I am not so naif as to think they are playing
Parcheesi. Specially since Ronnie has a knob on
the steering wheel, which means he is an expert
in driving with one hand!

Well, Leo, right after the Marv Griffin
Show last night, Bubbles confided something to
me that I will tell you verbatum, to get your remarks, positive or negative. Because I want to adopt
the best point of view for the future welfare of
my little girl. Here is how it went in words:

"Mom, I have a problem with Snakey!"

"Who is Snakey?" I ask the way any Mother
would upon hearing such a peculiar name for a human,
and not knowing if he walks or crawls.

"He is my best boy-friend!" said Bubbles.

"Does he walk or crawl?" I inquire.

"You are not funny!" protests Bubbles.
"Snakey is what all of we girls who know him call
Ronald Blish."

"So what is your exact problem?" I ask,
getting set for the worst kind of problem a 16 year
old jeune fille can have during these days when
boys and girls fool around with you-know-what in
ways my generation would never allow.

Now we go at it hammer and tongues:
Bubbles
"Well, Mum, Snakey is a passionate type,
being at that age—19. If you know what I mean."
Me
"I know what you mean. Don't."
Bubbles
"That is my problem! I have to tell you
that in spite of what you and Daddy think (the way
you both were always on my back) I have turned out
to be the strictly 'Moral' type!! I mean, I have
very strong in-hibitions. Like certain types of
places where I do not let a boy put his hands."
Me
"I am glad to hear that, darling. And I
respect you for it! I was a strict, 'moral' type
girl also, when I was your age. In fact, that is how
I landed your father, even though I would not call
him exactly a 'passionate' type. So I understand
you, dear . . . Is that what is disturbing your
sleep, mind, or ways of thought lately?"

<u>Bubbles</u>
"Yes. If you know what I mean."
<u>Me</u>
"O, I know what you mean, darling. In fact, there is little room for <u>not</u> knowing what you mean vis-a-vis that subject! It is the only subject the Male Sex has on their minds between the ages of 6 to 55, when they calm down—not because of moral principals or wanting to act like true gentlemen, but because Mother Nature, who happens to be female, decides when enough is enough!"
<u>Bubbles</u>
"Thanks a lot, Mom. You have been a great comfort to me is all I want to say."

And she kissed me and buzzed up to her room.

Well, Leo, that avoided the <u>real</u> question, of course, so I am appealing to you. What do you advise me to tell Bubbles the next time she broaches this subject—as I am sure she will?! How far <u>should</u> a "moral" girl who wants to stay popular with the opposing sex let a boy friend with certain urges "go"?

Frankly, I think that Mr. "Snakey" Blish is a real Don Coyote type, and is going to put the screws on our little girl any day now. If you ask me, they don't go around calling a boy "Snakey" without there being a very good reason for it! If you know what I mean.

Your thankful friend,

Florence ("Flo") Klitcher

P.S. <u>Mon dieu,</u> Leo, the problems a modern-type mother has to go through these awful days!!

LEO ROSTEN
Counsellor on Adenoids and Morals
309 Uptight Boulevard
Carnal Falls,
Louisiana

May 15

Mrs. Herman Klitcher
210 Placebo Park
Euphoria, Illinois 60035

Cher "Flo":

I certainly do know what you mean, Flo. In fact, I was once on exactly the same spot as Bubble's "B.F."—and a more miserable six months never gummed up my life. Let me give you the male point of view, and go on from there.

Back in my days at Crane Tech, I dated a very "moral" girl named Bavaria. One day, Bavaria asked me, "Was your father an octopus?"

"Why, no!" I protested. "What makes you ask a silly question like that?"

"The number of places on me you are trying to identify by touch," she replied.

Flo, I think you can see why I understand Bubbles's problem.

Let me offer some comments which may be helpful to you (and Herm) during the difficult period you are going through.

1) It is a well-established fact, among students of human behavior, that "moral" girls

cause "passionate" boys a great deal of anguish
and suffering.

2) Young men who have to contend with
"strictly moral" girls are even worse off. They
tend to come down with attacks of what psychiatrists
call "acute frustration." And careful research
shows that acute frustration can cause insomnia,
dandruff, or complete loss of appetite among young
males.

3) Girls, however, do not seem to develop
the same symptoms—perhaps because girls' sexual
needs are satisfied by substitute gratifications:
e.g., skipping rope, making Brownies, reading Edna
St. Vincent Malaise, or playing Run, Sheep, Run.

This leads me to the conclusion that you
and Hermie do not have to worry too much. If Bubbles
has had to stop Snakey from going too "far," it
means she was brought up right. It also means that
Snakey was, too—for he is simply showing all the
signs of being a fine, wholesome American boy, with
natural "urges" as patriotic as an exhibit in
Disneyland. Snakey may, in fact, be religious, and
is only trying to fulfill the Lord's injunction
to go forth and multiply. (I don't mean in arith-
metic, but in biology. What are his grades?)

If Bubbles could get Snakey to change his
nick-name (to, say, "Snoopy") half your troubles
might end right there.

Since you ask for practical advice, I
suggest you try the following: Take Bubbles aside
and tell her the following, in a warm, casual tone
of voice: "Honey, I am not going to lecture you
or try to change your private life. But as your
mother, who loves you regardless of anything—"
(pause a moment here, Flo, and let the lump form
visibly in your throat)—"I consider it my duty

to give you the benefit of my own experience . . .
If you let Snakey 'go' as far as he 'wants,' dear,
one of two things is sure to 'happen.' You will
either 1) regret it, or 2) enjoy it. In either case,
you will have a 'problem.' But"—(and this is the
important point to remember, Flo)"—you will
sleep a lot better."

      Do not add "And so will I and your father."

Votre ami,

Leo

P.S. I'm glad I'm not in Bubbles's shoes.

— *L. R.*

P.P.S. I'm even gladder I'm not in Ronald Blish's.

— *L*

Slats and
Dimples and
Chico and Toots

PENELOPE KLITCHER
210 Placebo Park
Euphoria,
Illinois 60035

May 12

Dear Mr. Roston—

     If my parents find out I am writing you—
and about <u>what</u>—O! Wow! The way things are going,
we are cooking up a storm in this funky home. The
reason is <u>they are too up-tight</u>—I mean Daddy and
Mom. They do not begin to even <u>dig</u> a girl such as I.
This is why I have to rip off to someone like I assume
you to be.

     Well, the fact is—I am in love! With a boy
who is just out of <u>sight!</u> Cool isn't the word for
him. He is the <u>Most!!</u> His name (you have to keep this
a secret) is Oscar Patuchik, but "Slats" is what
us girls all call him. "Slats" really turns me
on! And he says just my <u>picture</u> (in a real cute
Bikini) gives him the vibes. That is how we are about
each other. Like Wow! He is <u>the Greatest!</u> Terrif.

     "Slats" is 18 and I am 16 and as we are

both but zonked—<u>mad, mad,</u> MADLY in Love, why can't
we get married???

       <u>He</u> wants us to get our own pad as soon as I
graduate Shimmel High, but says he will go along
with my wishes in the matter and do "the Ring"
bit if that's the way it has to be it has to be.

       That's where it is, Mr. R.

       So what do you think?

       I know you are "with it"! in spite of
your age, because some of the things you write that
I have read are just fab! So please tell it like it
is.

"Penny" Klitcher

      (who <u>hates</u> being called "Bubbles")

P.S. Slats is <u>in no way</u> like Ronnie Blish, that nerd,
who my mother wrote you about (she let it slip out
last night.) We called Ronnie "Snake"—and was
he ever one, the rat! Some day I will tell you why
I say that!

from
Leo ("Fab") Rosten
Farout Boulevard
Rip Off
Tenn.

May 15

Dear "Penny":

I loved your fantastic letter, and am
honored to think that you trust me with your secret
—and even seek my opinion. I will gladly tell it
like it is.

According to authorities who are the greatest, being madly in love is a very good reason for
not getting married. Why? Because Love is a dangerous disease, Penny, marked by high fevers, far-out
illusions, bad English, and a complete paralysis
of cool. Marriage should only be undertaken in
cold blood.

These are the facts, Penny. Now, what do
I recommend to you in your (and "Slats's") present
state? That you both stay zonked—mad, mad, madly
in love—until the feeling passes over. Slats may
be 42 by that time, but you will undoubtedly be
married and have 2.5 children (which is the average
in the U.S.).

Yours,

Leo Boston

P.S. Do you dig?

"PENNY" KLITCHER
210 Placebo Park
Euphoria
Illinois, 60035

May 26

Dear Mr. R.—

I wish to thank you in person for all the
time and troubles you took to reply to me about my
plight. Thank you. (Your addresses are a blast!)

The way things have turned out, I did not
have to lay it on you after all. Because "Slats"
turned out to be a real Fink!! I have learned he was
"making out" with my best friend, "Dimples"
Zukerkandl, all the time he was giving me all that
jazz about my mere picture giving him the vibes!!

So we have split. Slats was a drag, I now
realise. Just the mere mention of that freak's
name tunes me out now. He is nothing but a forgotten
memory.

So I have recovered—and have put it all together. Because I have a new throb. Teddy ("Toots")
Towster. And is he something else again! Real cool,
and he lets it all hang out. He is not in any way like

Snakey or Slats—who each or both never really
"made the scene" with me. If you know what I mean.
So thank you for your interest which is
no longer necessary.

Your grateful friend

"*Penny*"

P.S. Mom does not know about "Toots"—so if she
asks you anything about my private life and you
write to her (or my Dad) please clam up. Just act
like Slats, Toots or Chico are Greek to you.

"*Penny*"

P.P.S. Chico is not a Greek, but Purto Ricon. He
is a real cute boy who although he tells everyone
I am his #1 Bird is only running #2 in my affection
at the present time.

<u>POST-MORTEM</u>
From
Leo Rosten

Dear "Penny":

 Right on.

    Your pen-pal

    — L. R.

Intermarriage:
Yes or No?

Cinderella LAMINATED SHIMS
83 Wacker Drive
Chicago, Illinois 60612

June 1

Leo Rosten
Apt. 39-A
Vesuvius Towers
644 E. 68 St.
New York, N.Y.

Dear Leo:

This will be short and brief as I am dashing
off to O'Hara Field to catch a plane to Detroit.
(Leo, do you realise O'Hara is the busyest airport
in the entire U.S.A.—a fact that you, as a former
native, have a right to be just as proud of as us!)
The reason I am heading for Detroit is that
I am in charge of plans for our Annual Sales Convention. Last year we performed Cinderellas annual
Pow-Wow in San Francisco—and Wow! what a Pow
we had there in 'Frisco!
But it is Detroit this year and no screwing
around—because the Pres. of the Co. (Flos father)
has laid down the law about his top people having
such a hot time and getting so crocked they dont
know Business vs. Pleasure. "Having a ball" is
O.K. in the right time and place, said Mr. Krumbach,
so long as it dont put a total cramp in conducting

business, that being the reason we are all there in the first place!

Just between you and I, Leo, what made Mr. Krumbach flip his lid was finding "Buck" Mutchlers wife in the shower in 418 with Jack ("Fly-by") Knight. The fact that both parties were fully in clothed, and not even starch naked (although "Mitzi" Mutschler was starting to approach that condition) did not subdue Mr. Krumbachs feelings 1 trifle.

So the next morning the Old Man took the roster (at our Breakfast Sing-and-meeting) and made a blister of a speech no one who heard it will ever forget! He said some guys spend more time getting stoned and swinging then Business at each years annual convention—and <u>dreaming</u> about the former during work-sessions of the later, when every loyal Cinderella man is suppose to give 100% to the subject under discussion and not doze off in horny memorys of the night before or the eve yet to come!

We might of <u>still</u> gotten the Old Geezer to relax a little and thus allow a Fun point of view— except that that night has to be the time "Googie" Conroy chooses to get bombed and parade down the 6th floor at 2 A.M. playing her G-- d--- gutar to stinko "Howie" Heffermans bawling "When Irish Eyes Are Smiling!"—and he is a Kraut, not 100 miles of being an Irishman (but gets just as cornball whenever swacked.) But 601-602 are Mr. Krumbachs suites. So that blew it for good! So long 'Frisco— Detroit, here we come.

Because Im still dashing to make that plane, lets get to the point of this missive—namely, <u>Do you beleive in Inter-Marriage?</u> (I mean between the colored races.)

This is not a gag, Leo, but a real tough business problem we have! With the type salesmen we get these days (in the growing market for homes and therefore laminated shims) houses are going up right and left like wildfires—many of them in neighborhoods where "Segregation" has not arrived (the land being empty before those houses are put up there). And the new bread of salesman are not exactly shy about controvertial subjects. They do not stall around about hitting right to the gut in our "bull sessions"—however "delicate" that point might be. And <u>"Race" in housing is very big this year!</u>

Thats why I want to pick your brains in advance. I desire to straiten out my own thinking sos I am prepared in case some wisenheimer in our mist throws Mr. Pulsifer (our V.P. who I work under) a slider. I have to back up Mr. Pulsifer 100% if he gets in a 3-and-2 spot!

So that is why I desire your best answer to—Do <u>you</u> beleive in Inter-Marriage?

I sure appreciate your answer to this burning tissue.

Your old buddy,

"Herm"

P.S. Send your answer to my office (83 Wacker Drive, Chi.) as I will only be planning ahead in Detroit 2-3 days depending on weather—I mean <u>wether</u> Flo will come up during them (ha, ha)!

P.P.S. I had to give the heave-ho to Miss Farfadetto, after we find to our horrors that she has filed all our correspondents with U.S. Steel under "Government".

So I have a new "Tempo" who looks O.K. as a girl Friday. She takes shorthand! (Altho it is some time before I get it back.)

The only thing is that Flo hasnt seen this piece of cake yet. Man. She wears a Mini-Skirt so high you cant tell if its a skirt or a belt. Every time she sits down all the men stand up—and not because the Flag is passing. This cup-cake doesnt wear no "bra" neither, so when she walks to or fro it is like she is made of Jello. Man.

"Herm"

LEO ROSTEN
Specialist on Desegregation
14 Spectrum Street
Rainbow Falls
Vermont

June 5

Herman P. Klitcher
Cinderella Laminated Shims, Inc.
83 Wacker Drive
Chicago, Ill. 60612

Dear Herm:

Do I believe in Inter-marriage? Absolutely
not! Most of the world's problems can be traced to
the fact that members of the male and female races
keep marrying each other.

There is only one argument in favor of
inter-marriage, Herm: It's more fun than any other
type of inter-racial activity.

Now, I realize that not everyone is built
the way I am (42, 37, 39). Some of the smartest people
I know do not believe in marriage at all. Others
believe in marriage as an institution, but say they
don't want to live in one (ha, ha).

Excuse this hasty response to your epistle.
I am catching the night plane to Rhodesia.

Yours,

Leo

P.S. Is your "tempo" happy in laminated shims?
I know an author in New York who is looking for a
girl Friday, Saturday or Sunday. He uses long-hand.
Man.

**From the Desk of
Herman P. Klitcher**

June 8

Dear Leo—

My "Tempo" <u>had</u> the name of "Bebe"
Krauss. And she never worked on Friday (or Monday
as well).

I say she "had" that handle on account of
the very day we got back from the pow-wow in Detroit
Mr. Pulsifer asks me to let "Bebe" help him out
with his very heavy work lode—by staying in the
office over-time. (Ha, ha.)

But it so happened Mr. Krumbach was working
over-time as well, and he took 1 gander at those
bouncing cantalopes and gave "Bebe" the Bye-Bye.
Then he called the Tempo Sec. Agency and asked if they
were supplyers of Secretarys or Sexertainers! (When
that old poop gets mad he can curl your hairs with
sarcasms.)

So I now have a new steno—right out of
Wistlers Mothers rocker. Her name is Mabel Pencil.
Can you tie that??

"Herm"

P.S. Mr. Pulsifer is now selling plastic flowers
in jolly Joliet.

The Seven
Wonders of
the World

Mrs. Herman P. Klitcher
201 Placebo Park
Euphoria, Ill. 60035

June 11

Dear <u>Cher Ami</u> Leo—

We had the Gang in for a Buffet Supper last
night (Sunday, it so happens, altho I sometimes
do the same informal-type entertaining in the after-
noons). It was a real Fun Party! The hi-light was
our playing "The Game"—or as you and I called
it when I was a <u>jeune fils</u>—"Charades." I am sure
you must be one of the worlds' best players of that,
with your vocabulery, education, past knowledge,
and so forth.

Well, one of the "act-outs" of words
that Hermie, me and "Tubby" and "Dotty" Wunach
(who made up our team of 4 players each) got was—
"The 7 Wonders of the World." Leo, we got that in
like 1 min. 10 seconds! Our opponements (the Felix
Kupfers plus Buddy and Orpheus Botnovik) were fools
to give us such an easy thing to act out.

But now comes the interesting part—what
transpired <u>afters.</u> Andy Shüssel asked us all what
actually <u>are</u> (or were) each of those "7 Wonders of
the World."?!!

Well, Leo, you should of seen the peculier
things some people nominated for a Wonder! (Like

106

the Washington Monument or Niagara Falls—which
were not even <u>built</u> at the time whoever chose "The
7 Wonders of the World" chose them.) And the argument we had because not one single person of all of
our whole crowd could name all the 7 of them will go
down as one of the best we ever had in Euphoria.

Mortie Freibush (the famous Suspants distributor of that name) said he was <u>sure</u> "Nero's
Burning of Rome" was one of the 7 wonders. But
"Bunny" Gliship who belongs to three Book Clubs
said that was silly, a Burning being a <u>disaster</u> and
not a Wonder. I was on her side.

Our agreed nominations for the 7 Wonders
were—
1) The Hanging Gardens in Bologna
2) The Coliseum of Roads
3) Socrates'es affair with Cleopatra
4) The Vested Virgins of Rome
—and these (or those) are all the wonders we could
agree about! And even on them, there was plenty of
argument with no one <u>sure</u> he or she are 100% in the
right!

That is why I am sending you this <u>billet.</u>
Please do us all a big favor, Leo (it will only take
a few minutes I know) and without jestery just jot
down the correct "7 Wonders of the World" by return
Mail.

<u>Merci</u> a million!

Your friend,

Florence ("Flo") Klitcher

P.S. Can you answer fast? I want to surprise the Gang

at "Buzz" and Olga Shlimhoff's 20-th anniversary
(wedding) on the 18-th of next month.

The Shlimhoffs are a drag, <u>entre nous,</u> and
embarass us by their squabbeling at the drop of a
hat. That is why some one (of our Gang) always tries
to liven up a Shlimhoff party with another game
we all love, namely, "20 Questions"—which is
just right for a 20th Anniversary, and has become
a kind of tradition here in Euphoria for couples
celebrating their 20-th.

I would like to stump one-and-all by having
as my "20 Questions" secret a "7-th Wonder of
the World" they never heard of!! <u>Touchez?</u>

"Flo"

Mr. Leo Rosten
Apt. 39-A
Vesuvius Towers
644 E. 68th St.
New York, N.Y. 10022

LEO ROSTEN
Memory Expert & Researcher
54 Mnemonic Peak
Encyclopedia Universal
Ojai
Spain

June 14

Cher Flo:

Touchez.

Nero's burning Rome was definitely not one
of the "Seven Wonders of the World." It was one of
the Seven Boo-Boos of the World, and Morty Freibush
should be ashamed of himself for nominating it.

Neither (I regret to tell you) was Socrates'
affair with Cleopatra. Cleopatra lived so many
years after Socrates that the only way he could get
at her was by short wave, which they did not have at
the time (and is sexually unsatisfactory as well).

But some of your gang's other answers came
pretty close to the truth. Experts agree that the
"Seven Wonders of the World" really were:

   1) The Hanging Gardens of Babylon
       (the Bologna ploy is sheer balo-
       ney)
   2) The Statue of Colossus in Rhodes
       (that was a big wonder)
   3) The Pyramids
       (which are still there, unlike
       #1 and #2)
   4) The Leaning Tower of Pizza

5) The Democratic Convention which nom-
    inated George McGovern.
6) The Watergate Fantods.

                  Your friend,

                    Leo

P.S. Have a Fun Time at the Shlimhoff's.

Just A Reminder .!?
from
Florence ("Flo") Klitcher

<u>Cher</u> Leo:

      Your list of the "7 Wonders of the World"
is 1 wonder short!!

               <u>Brusquement</u> (in haste)

                   "Flo"

Just A RIPOSTE
from
Leo ("Clip") Rosten

<u>Cher ami</u> Flo:

That is correct.

Hastily <u>(avec précipité)</u>

Leo

Just A Reminder .!?
from
Florence ("Flo") Klitcher

June 15

Dear Leo:

I <u>know</u> it is correct (7 being one more than 6, which is the number of "wonders" you submitted)!

My problem is—What do I tell the gang if some-one asks me (as some joker in that crowd is sure to) to name <u>all of the 7 wonders beside the 4 I will have ready</u>?!

<u>Votre ami,</u>

"Flo"

P.S. I say I will only have "4" ready because the 7 Wonders were of old—whereas the Demo. Convention occurred in 1972! (That shrinks your list to 5.) And <u>apropos</u> of the Watergate "fantods"—I will not even comment on your feeble humor re that (which cuts down your list to 4.)

So: can you send me 3 more wonders? Or at least just the 7th???

"Flo"

<u>Cher</u> Flo:

  Tell them you are saving the seventh wonder
of the world for the Shlimhoff's <u>50th</u> wedding anniversary. That ought to stop any joker who chal-
lenges you—because judging from one or two things
you let drop in a previous letter, it will be a miracle if "Buzz" and Olga are still a twosome for
their 21st.

  In fact, if anyone crowds you, say that that
will be the seventh wonder.

         Votre ami,

         Leo

A THANK YOU NOTE FROM FLORENCE ("FLO") KLITCHER

<u>Mon cher, cher ami—</u>

     You are a doll! A living doll!! With a
<u>riposte</u> like that, whoever nags me at the Shlimhoff
blow-out to name the 7th Wonder (of the World) will
have egg on his face for the remainder of the fes-
tival!

                       <u>Merci beaucoup,</u>

                          "Flo"

P.S. Is Bologne (Italy) <u>really</u> where baloney was
discovered? What a store-house of peculier information your mind is made of!

Dear cher Flo:

Bologna was named "Bologna" (in 1573)
after 16 historic scrolls of baloney were found
in dry caves outside that city. In fact it was the
discovery of those scrolls that started archaeologists digging all over the map.

When the map failed to provide any useful
artifacts, the archaeologists began excavating
earth. So many died in the cause of science, that
Pope Sixtus V named one part of the globe in their
honor.

Toujours yours,

Leo

Follow-Up from "Herm"

Dear Leo—

    Cheese and crackers, pal! Flo showed me your
latest correspondents, and I have to say you have
us both going in <u>circels!</u> You are the living end!

    That screwball stuff about "Balogna" and
"baloney" is for the <u>birds,</u> which we are not!

              Your pal in spite of that,

                "Herm"

P.S. I dare you tell—what part of the globe did that
Pope name in honor of those departed diggers of
yore??!

<u>FAREWELL</u>
from
"<u>Leo</u>"

Dear Herm:

    The Dead See.

Leo

You, Too,
Can Write
a Best-Seller

July 10

Leo Rosten
Apt. 39-A
Vesuvius House
644 East 68th St.
New York, New York

Dear Leo:

It sure has been a long time since I have
not written you. But now I have a real hot idea.

Yesterday, persuing the Sundays paper,
my eyes happened to fall on the "Book Page" of the
<u>Trib</u> (which as you know is the largest paper not only
in Chi. but <u>in the entire Mid-West)</u> and I noticed
something that made my eyes pop right out of their
socks. Your latest new book—right up there on the
<u>Best-Seller-Lists!!</u>

I bet you will stash away 1,000,000 bucks
(or "simoleons" as we used to say at old Crane
Tech.) Wow, Leo, 1,000,000 clams! Congrats!!

So that set me thinking. You may not know
it, Leo, but I once took a crack at authorship myself
(I admit that someone usualy had to clean up my
spelling, which as you know I was not a whiz at like
you.)

After we went our separate pathways from

Crane Tech, I entered Theodore Roosevelt Jun. Coll.
I dont want to brag, but I wrote maybe 20-30 items
for the Roosevelt <u>Bully</u>, our school weekly. And
you would of been amazed how many people came up to
me crying "Hey, what have we here in our mist—
another John Steinberg?" The people on my fathers
side were even more complimenting.

So why didnt I go on into authorship as a full
time job, you may ask? Because I met "Flo," who
you never had the pleasure of meeting. Her name
at that time was Florence Krumbach and her old man
owns Cinderella Laminated Shims which he is also the
founder of. After taking the vows of holy matri-
money, I worked my a-- off, and with no help from
anyone worked up to Asst. Mgr. of Mid-west Sales,
which includes all of Chicago, the largest city in
Illinois, plus areas right down to Omoha and up to
Minneapolis.

But frankly, Leo (and I hope you keep this
to yourself) my heart is not in laminated shims.

So—as I am in the Prime Time of Life, and
with plenty of zing to go around, do you think it is
too late for me and try to crack the big time as a
Writer?

Last night I tossed this idea off to Flo,
telling her how you have just banged out a Best-
Seller you can salt away maybe 1 million clams from.
And man, did I get a re-action! She (Flo) lit up like
a house on fire with "That is a <u>dandy</u> idea! Why dont
you ask Leo to give you the inside dope on what tricks
to use as a writer? As a "Pro" he must know all
kinds of secrets of that trade. And if anyone wants
to adorn the Literary Seen, they should write best-
sellers and not waste their time on just any type
book!" Which sure is true.

So I would apreciate the lowdown on how to

turn out a Best-seller. I am not spit-balling about
this, Leo, because I want to write badly. I am ready
to give 2 nights a week and every Sat. aft. to this.

Perhaps you are wondering do I have anything
specific in mind, plot-wise? Well, I sure do! Listen
to this story I dreamed up—and I <u>know</u> it can ring
the bell money-wise:

A war-hero P.O.W. from Vietnam (Jack
Marlow) comes home to Waukegan, Illinois, and there
he sees his kid brother (Sherman) has this gorgeous,
beautiful girl—named Shirley, who our hero falls
in love with like a ton of bricks. But Jack hates to
break his kid brothers heart by stealing his girl
away from him, so he says <u>nothing,</u> but suffers and
suffers in noble silences.

Now, here comes my twist! The kid brother
(Sherman) who never dreamed he was queer, suddenly
feels in love with his best friend, Trevor.

So Sherman asks Jack to break this news to
Shirley (his intended)—and that their Love has to
be over! So Jack tells her. He even tells her <u>why,</u>
it not being a crime for someone like Sherman (who
even as a kid liked to play with dolls and use lip-
stick) to end up "going for" a boy of his own sex
instead of a girl of the others.

Well, I don't have to tell you how this makes
Shirley cry!! But through her bawling (which anyone who is hep to what is going on all around us in
re sex hang-ups can understand) she (Shirley) lets a
new angel slip out: "I never understood before why
Sherm painted his toe-nails!"

"How do you know that?" Jack amazes.

"I noticed it at the beach" weeps Shirley "and should of suspected he was not all
"straight" in the sex dept.!"

Well <u>this</u> gives Jack the right to pop some-

thing he would never in 1,000 years before confess.
"But I love you Shirl, with all my heart and sole.
I fell heads over heel for you the minute I laid my 2
eyes on you! Will you marry me?! Before any priest,
minister or rabbi of your own choice!"

So they get together. (And if it is a mixed
marriage, like her being Catholic and him Baptist,
or even him Gentile and her of the Jewish fate,
there is the extra element of Tolerance that is so
popular today when even a Protestent-to-Catholic
match is kosher.)

Leo, you have to admit that a story about 2
brothers in love with the same girl and 1 of them
turns out to be a "fag" is surefire today at the
box-office! Especially if Sherman and Trevor get
married! (We had a case like that in nearby Kenosha!)

How does this grab you??

How much money should I ask the publisher
to pony up? I hear some of them take the lion's share
of the stick leaving the Author the short hair.

Well, pal, I will sign off now and hope you
make a mint on your new book! And if you want to send
Flo and I an Autograph copy we wont return it—ha,
ha, ha.

Please answer right a way. Because I'm
roaring to go! And will be watching these good old
U.S. mails!!!

Your old buddy,

Herman ("Herm") Klitcher

P.S. Do not pull your punches, Leo. You can give it

to me straight. I can take it, if I want to be a
"Pro" writer.

"Herm"

P.P.S. The Trib also hinted you will sell your book
to Hollywood, so Flo asked me did you always have a
yen to write for the Silver Screen? Or did some 1
dramatic experience make you decide to live by the
pen?

"H"

LEO ROSTEN
Multi-Millionaire Author
77 Croesus Palisades
Eldorado
Oklahoma

July 20

Herman Klitcher
Cinderella Laminated Shims
83 Wacker Drive
Chicago, Ill. 60612

Dear Herm:

You would be surprised by how many old pals,
from whom I have not heard in ages, have written to
express their affection and concern for my health
since my book became a best-seller. Some even offer
to help me with my taxes, agreeing to become depen-
dents, whose monetary support is tax deductible.
There are no friends like old friends.

Herm, I know I can level with you when I say
that although my book is a best-seller, $1,000,000
is actually $130 more than I can expect to earn from
it. This is just one example of the disappointments
a "pro" writer runs into. One of America's leading
authors is still in a depression because the royal-
ties from his last novel came to within a few cents
of a fabulous fortune.

Your wife Flo was right on the ball when she
told you not to write just any book but to concentrate on best-sellers. Careful research has proved

(and this is confidential, Herm) that best-sellers sell more copies than any other type of book!

It is hard for me to comment upon your story, because ever since reading it I have had tears in my eyes. It "grabbed" me so hard I can't eat anything except soft food.

Instead, I'll answer Flo's request for the "inside dope" on authorship. I don't mind doing this—if you promise not to go around blabbing these professional secrets to everyone in Euphoria. After all, Herm, we don't want every joker in the U.S. knocking off a best-seller whenever he feels like it. I rely on you to keep the following hot tips to yourself:

1) To be a "pro" writer take the positive approach to a subject, like <u>How to Strike Oil in Your Back Yard</u> or <u>100 Ways to Beat the Odds at Monte Carlo.</u>

To be a <u>con</u> writer, on the other hand, concentrate on negative subjects, such as:
<u>God Is Dead—So Why Aren't You?</u>
<u>How I Caught My Shirt in a Xerox Machine</u>
         <u>and Was Arrested by the F.B.I.</u>
<u>Stamp Out Armenian Mezzuzahs!</u>
These titles are just examples.

2) Get a snappy title for your book. If you will study the names of recent best-sellers, you will see how snappy they are: <u>Jonathan Livingston Seagull,</u> for instance. (The publishers wanted to call it <u>Jonathan Livingston Siegel,</u> to attract Jewish buyers, but the author, Johann Bach, was a pretty shrewd customer and would not budge.)

I do not mind giving you some sure-fire titles as starters:
<u>A Parent's Guide to Nail-Biting</u>
<u>Oedipus-Shmoedipus, Just So You</u>
         <u>Remember Mother's Day</u>

The Tallest Midget in Texas

3) If you can't find a snappy title, Herm, choose a romantic or alluring one. Remember How to Avoid Probate? That was a blockbuster, and it was not even written by a "pro," but by a fellow who wrote only on weak ends and Halloween.

Another sure-fire title is: Sex Is the Most Fun You Can Have Without Laughing, but that's not original, ha, ha.

4) Choose a clean, wholesome plot—about children's toys, say, like The Valley of the Dolls. Or write up the sweet, uncomplicated way of life in a small town, like Peyton Place. And there's always room for a folksy story about marriage, like Who's Afraid of Edward Albee?

5) Avoid depressing titles, Herm. Portnoy's Complaint, for instance, could have been a best-seller (instead of laying an egg) if the title had been Portnoy's Delight or Ship Ahoy with Al Portnoy. The same goes for Death of A Salesman— a very depressing title—which could have run 3-4 months on Broadway if it had only had a more up-beat title, like The Song of Willy Loman or Fun and Frolic on the Open Road.

6) Choose a classy pen name. I don't want to hurt your feelings, Herm, but to be perfectly frank about it, "Herman P. Klitcher" is not the best name for a writer of best-sellers. That might go with a title like You and Your Fly-Wheel, but not for the type of story you sent me a synopsis of.

Many "big-time" writers use pen names, you know: for instance, John O'Hara, whose real name was Sol Rabinowitz. (I hope you will not let this get around.)

I have thought up a pen name for you that will guarantee you a best-seller: "Dr. Spock."

Some people think "Dr. Spock" is the pen name used by Truman Capote, but that's not true; Truman's nom de plume, as we pros call it, is "Jacqueline Susann." And I don't have to tell what a hit that made.

7) Use a typewriter in which the carriage moves from left to right, not from right to left. You really have to watch out for that these days, Herm, because Arab governments are smuggling Muslim typewriters into our stores like crazy. Muslim typewriters move from right to left. One writer I know was tricked into buying a Libyan typewriter last year and his book sold only 43 copies in the U.S. He still cannot figure out why it was a smash in Cairo.

8) When you write, do it by daylight or electricity. Do not use candles, except when writing ghost stories. Never write by flashlight, because the batteries have to be changed too often, and few authors know how to change the batteries in a flashlight without cutting their fingers to the bone. A writer who has cut his fingers to the bone finds it very hard to ring the bell.

9) At the end of your book, be sure to write "THE END." This is very important, Herm. If you don't write "THE END," many a reader will go right on reading into the blank end-pages, and will conclude that you did not have anything more to say. That could ruin your chances for a best-seller.

Besides, we know that many women absent-mindedly put their shopping lists or overdue bills in the back of whatever book they're reading, and if they go past the end and read them, thinking them part of the story, they get pretty confused. My Aunt Molly was recently absorbed in a novel by P. J. Wodehouse about a missionary in the South Seas who, in-

stead of converting the natives, becomes a cannibal
himself. But Wodehouse had forgotten to put "THE
END" at the conclusion of his tale, and my Aunt,
who had stuck a bill for a fertilizer-spreader from
Sears in the back of the book, read that, assuming
it was part of the story. She told me she just loved
the story up to the very conclusion—where, she
said indignantly, the author dodged the real issue.

Now let's turn to what you should do after
your book has been published. Publicizing a book
after it has been published is what makes best-
sellers these days. In fact, some writers spend
more time promoting their books than writing them.
Here are some hot tips.

1) Sue Louis Nizer. Mr. Nizer has made a
fortune writing about clients whom he had defended
in court; but no one ever thought of suing him! Pro-
motion-wise, Herm, nothing could be nizer.

2) Get the CIA to buy 1,000 copies of your
book. If they don't want to buy a thousand copies
(although I can't see why not, considering all the
other things they do) send them 1,000 copies—and
tip off the gossip columns. Between the CIA's
denials and Jack Anderson's exposés you will get
$10,000,000 worth of free publicity.

3) Announce that you wrote your book while
under the influence of marijuana, "speed," or LSD.
That will get you on all the television "talk
shows." If LSD makes you break out in pimples, start
a rumor that you married a dwarf: that will get you
on David Susskind.

You asked me about publishers' advances.
Herm, you must realize that book publishers are very
kind men who hate to "pony up" a huge advance because that only puts the writer in a higher tax
bracket. My publisher nets only 2 cents on each

book he sells, which he donates to the Metropolitan
Life Insurance Company. My share is 1 cent. When I
asked him, "How come I only get a penny a copy?"
he answered, "That's a good question."

That about wraps it up, Herm. Once you have
written a best-seller, you and Flo will get a big
kick out of all the fan mail: for money, your autograph, money, a lock of hair, money, your photograph, donations to the Home for Tuba Players Who
Fall Down Dry Wells, money—or from child psychologists who think that the pop-snap-crackle noises
made by morning cereals is making our children
neurotic. You will even receive letters from old
friends who want to write badly—and do.

I hope you won't forget me after you hit the
best-seller lists, pal. If you don't, send me some
autographed laminated shims. The ones I own burn a
lot of oil. I don't have to tell you how a creative
writer hates the smell of burning laminated shims.
It keeps him from writing another best-seller.

Sincerely,

Leo Rosten

P.S. Flo asks did I always want to write movies, or
"did some one dramatic experience" make me decide
"to live by the pen"? Tell her I had one very
dramatic experience, which I have never before
breathed to a living soul.

Back in the 1960's, I dropped in on
"Pinsky's Halvah Heaven," a little Chinese restaurant off Mosholu Parkway, and when I opened my
fortune cookie, I found that the rice-paper inside

contained a synopsis for a perfect screenplay for
Elvis Presley and Yvonne de Carlo. I considered this
a good omen. So I quickly expanded on the contents
of the cookie, writing in a juicy part for Howard
Hughes. (I happened to know that Hughes, who had
just bought the Gulf Stream, was dying to play the
role of a man who was faking the life story of Clif-
ford Irving.)

      I rushed my manuscript to a Hollywood agent
whose offices are next door to a blood bank. The
agent dashed over to Paramour Pictures, and within
twenty minutes, Herm, received a bid of $463,000!
I wanted to hold out for $465,000, but the agent,
who has a branch in Tel Aviv, told me not to be a pig.
Right then and there I knew I could live by the pen.

**From the Desk of
Herman P. Klitcher**

July 26

Dear Leo:

Whats the name of your agent?

"Herm"

Zeno's Paradox
Solved at
Last!

Cinderella LAMINATED SHIMS
83 Wacker Drive
Chicago, Illinois 60612

Sept 20

Leo Rosten
Apt. 39-A
Vesuvius Towers
644 E. 68 St.
New York, N.Y. 10021

Dear Leo:

I sure hope you had a good summer, as I did
not write you. But here we go again! Not that I want
to be a pest to a guy as busy and with more important
things to do as you are. But I frankly just dont know
where else I can turn to!
This is in regard to my son Alvin—and
Dad-Son relations. (I sure wish I could <u>dictate</u> this
whole shmeer to a Secretary instead of me hunt-and-
pecking away, but I am minus a Sec.—as Flos old
man fired mine, a real looker with gordgeous bal-
loons baring the name of Ursula Sabatini, on account
of every time she sashayed to the water-cooler the
male staff could not keep their minds on laminated
shims.)
What I started out to ask you is about my
son Alvin and his problem—which he has to dump in
my lap, as usual. The Shimmel High Seniors here
have 1 rotten teacher, the mean type who just loves

to try and trip them up on exams. His name is Mr. Wambsganss. Resently he told that class as follows: "Well, Senior boys and girls, soon you will be out of Shimmel, and some of you will aspire to a college of your choice—if they take you in. Or you will go to #2, 3, 4 on your list. So listen hard, kids, because this may be the turning point in your life!!

"I happen to know that in your Coll. Entrance Board exams you might run into some smart-Alec type question, regarding what they call "Zero's Paradox". This is a real stopper, kids, so brace yourselfs.

"This Zero was a Greek, way back when they sat around in that part of the world with nothing to do except try to stump each other with hair-spliting type useless questions (while the other Greeks, who were named Spartns, were on the ball all the time, exercising, sparring, bilding up their strenth and getting in shape for war against each other).

"Well, this one Greek by the name of Zero, to keep up with the other Big Brains like Soccerates and Acropolis, made the flat statement (hold your hat, pal!) that there is no such thing as Moving!

"I dont mean moving from 1 address to another (said Mr. Wambsganss, whos peculier name you will recognize if you think about it as the same as the guy who made the only unassissted Triple Play in Worlds Series History!) I mean Motion! Even slow motion is not possible (said Zero). Motion is just 1 of the many false Illusions we poor mortals are prone to. Motion is not a fact but a false error, no matter what our own 2 eyes say about that.

To "prove" this cockamamy idea, said Mr. W., this smart-ass Zero dreamed up the following race: "Take the fastest runner in all of the Greek aisles,

and put him up against a porpoise—but give the
porpoise a 10-yards head-start. Okay? Well, Zero
said that no Greek athalete could ever catch up
with that porpoise, no matter how fast he (the
Greek) runs! And WHY?! This is where we hit the
Paradox.

Because plain "Logic" proves (acc. to
Zero) that before the human Greek can even reach
the turtle, he has to reach ½ the distance between
him and the crawler. O.K. But during that time,
the porpoise has moved farther on, right? So now
the Greek track-star has to cover ½ of that distance, too—but meanwhile the turtle has moved
still farther! So the Greek has to cover ½ of that
space—and so on and so on until your mind gets
dizzy trying to figure out the joker in this cockamamy proposition.

Zero said no Greek athalete can never catch
up with his turtles if you give them an inch! As
for passing them—that is out of the question alltogether,

Dont tell me this isnt a killer, logic-
wise, Leo.

To put it in another (and even more heart-
burn way)—Before you or me or anyone can take a
step—just a step, like 1 foot—he has to step 6"
(½ of 1 foot). But before he can step 6" he has to
step 3"! (½ of 6). And before he can reach 3" he has
to get to 1-½". And etc. So you come back smack to
the fact that we cant even move at all (if you listen
to Zeros type of fact twisting!!)

So—where does that leave us? Any dumbell
knows from his own common sense that we mortals
do actualy move around all the time. Even babies
crawl from 1 place to another, and they never even

heard of Zero and could not tell you what a Paradox
is (maybe that is why they get around.)

Anyway, that is what put the whole senior
class at Shimmel in a mental shambels, with Alvin
in the lead.

Naturaly, Alvin can hardly wait to get home
and dump the problem in guess whos lap?? Right!
Me. In front of Flo and the other children.

Well, no sooner does Alvin get thru de-
scribing Zero's made-up baloney than I exclaim
"That is not logic but Bubblegum!"

"Do not duck the point of the problem"
protests Alvin "which is how do you prove by pure
reason that you or anyone else can move!"

"By useing the 2 eyes God gave you and not
have a pile of wool pulled over them!" I respond
"Any dummy can use his own horse-sense and see that
in real life we do get to where we want from where
we were. (And I suppose horse-sense does not apply
to porpoises or turtles, I crack!). The human race
doesnt just stand around paralyze, like in Madame
Trouseaus Museum in London. Motion is going on
around us every single second, for C----- sake!
Like this!" And I swing my arm around 180 degrees
(and nock Flos favorite vase off the fireplace
mantel, but figure it is worth it in the cause of
Education.) "You miss the whole point!" hollers
Alvin. "The problem is not in doing but in Reasoning
—proving by your powers of analyzing that you
can move! Zero says you only think you do but cant
prove it."

"I just proved it!" I proclaim.

"But in action, not Logic!" jabbers Alvin.

"I do not have to prove in logic what I
show in action!" I shoot back.

"That is ducking Zero's question!"
Alvin repeats. "Take it again, Daddy-O. If the
athalete has to get to ½ of his destination, he
first has to get to ¼ —and before that he has to—"

"That is a <u>fasinating</u> problem!" now pops
Penelope, before I can brain her.

"It makes a chill run up and down my spine"
offers Mildred, but with sarcasm (tho she is the
usualy the first to join Alvin in any Contempt-
for-Dads I.Q. routine.)

"<u>I</u> think it is nuts" says Hortense.

But now Flo has to butt in, irregardles
of my feelings—"If that was a nutty problem,
Mr. Wambsganss would of said so and not procede to
torture the Senior class with it!!"

"Right on!" says Alvin.

"So whats the answer, Pop?" grins Mildred,
showing her true colors.

"Put up or shut up" chimes in Flo "as
the kids say."

Well, Leo, I bust out in a sweat, so what
can I do except stall—"I am thinking."

"Think how you are copping out" murmurs
Mildred.

"Watch your English!" I retort.

"The problem is not in English but in
Logic" says Alvin.

"Get off Daddys back" observes Hortense.

"According to Zero I cant even get ½ way
up his back!" cracks Alvin.

Now I stare at Alvin with all the indiginity
a Father can bring into action at a time like that.
"That Zero stuff is a trick question!" I decide
"there is a catch in it."

"Where?" persists Alvin.

"I will find it" I say.

"I might not live that long" cracks Alvin.

"Go to your room!" I command.

"Why are you picking on Alvin?" demands Penelope.

"Go to your room" I inform her.

"You are mad because you dont know the answer!" crys Mildred (a switch-hitter.)

"Go to your room!" I rule.

"Listen, sweet-heart" busts in Flo "I did not take my marriage vows to one by the name of Adolf Hitler!" And she stawks out of the room.

"Good night Hitler" yaps Hortense in exiting as well.

So there I am, Leo—with supper on the table for 6 people and only I to consume it. Which I do.

I am up ½ the night with acid indigestion and G-- only knows what else from so much grub on top of personal shame and humilliation.

Well, that was 2 nights ago, Leo, and I am still not back to normal. Because I am still in a jam (I mean about answering Zero). All 5 of my own flash-and-blood keep regarding me like I am a $3 bill. If you know what I mean.

"Take your time, Daddy (or "Honey") they croon, dripping sarcasm like it was maple syrup.

That is the reason for this long epistle.

Please, Leo do not kiss it off (as has been your way with 1 or 2 other appeals for help I made to you). This Zero is a ball-buster, so far as Yours Truly is conserned.

I know you will rush to my side—even with a short note which gives me the dope to answer the 2 basic problems—

1) Was that Greek creep pulling a fasty?

2) <u>How do I demolish Alvin?</u>

Hurry.

Your old buddy

" *Herm* "

P.S. I did come up with 1 idea—but want to check it
out with you first. <u>What if that race was held back-</u>
<u>wards ??</u> I mean, if you cant prove that Moving is
possible <u>forwards</u> is no reason it might not take
place <u>backwards!!</u>

 Do you think that answer will go over with
Mr. Wambsganss??

LEO ROSTEN
Logician
142 Paradox Gulch
Athens
Kentucky

Sept. 26

Herman P. Klitcher
Cinderella Laminated Shims, Inc.
83 Wacker Drive
Chicago, Ill. 60612

Dear Herm:

After reading your letter, I have not slept much either. Stories like yours go a long way toward explaining what is wrong with family life in America today.

I have good news, Herm! It happens that I solved Zeno's Paradox years ago; you will have no trouble with it from now on.

First, tell Alvin he has goofed up two entirely different men: Zero and Zeno. The former was an Assyrian who discovered nothing, perhaps the most useful idea in mathematics; but the latter, Zeno (the one Mr. Wambsganss had in mind), was the unemployed philosopher who made up the classic puzzler about Achilles and the tortoise. That was not the only paradox Zeno cooked up. (That fellow was a whiz, Herm, at driving people off their rockers.) For instance:

1) The Arrow Paradox. Zeno argued that

an arrow, "going" from its bow to its target, is actually at rest at any given point between that bow and that target. And if it is at rest, it is not moving. Therefore, it never moves at all. It is just an arrow, Herm, standing still in mid-air, on one spot after another. I know this is hard to believe, Herm.

In fact, other Greek philosophers did not believe it either. Zeno's opponents said that what that taffy-head had really proved is that there is no arrow—just the flight. Another school took a third position, maintaining that it is ridiculous to say there is no arrow or no flight, because we damn well observe both. They said there was no Zeno.

You are in pretty good company, Herm.

2) Zeno and Determinism

Zeno believed in predestination—arguing that everything we do is not freely chosen but has been pre-determined, before we were born.

One day, Zeno's slave, a Cretan named Yonklowitz, did something bad, and Zeno clobbered him. Yonklowitz cried, "But, master, according to your philosophy I was destined to do that; so why blame me?"

Kind Zeno replied, "I do not blame you, Yonklowitz, I whack you—because that is what I was pre-destined to do."

This story might come in handy, Herm—say with Alvin.

3) Zeno and No Motion

I say: If motion is not possible, how could Zeno move his vocal cords to say that? This is called Rosten's Clincher, and has made me the idol of philosophy students from Kansas to Khartoum.

To return to your problem: the biggest corker Zeno pulled, about the tortoise and the hare (or Achilles and the tortoise). Buddy, you can easily turn the tables on Zeno—and give Alvin, Mildred, Penelope, Hortense and your wife Flo the come-uppance they deserve. Here is how to explain it:

Say you live in Chicago. You want to go to St. Louis. Zeno says you can't. Well, you go down to Union Station and in a loud, firm voice announce: "I want to buy a ticket to Los Angeles!"

According to Zeno, you can't get to Los Angeles without first reaching St. Louis. Fine. Get off right there.

It's as simple as that, Herm.

Your pal

Leo

P.S. You can even get a rebate for the unused part of your ticket.

**From the Desk of
Herman P. Klitcher**

Sept. 29

Dear Leo:

You are a real genius!

Man, did I ever let Alvin, Flo, "Bubbles"
etc. have it right between the eyes (in re Zeno
and his "paradox.")

Alvin has just told me that Mr. Wambsganss
turned as pale as a sheet when he (Alvin) spouted
that answer in class!!

Thanks a million, pal. You are the greatest!

"*Herm*"

P.S. How would I get back to Chicago? I mean from
St. Louis.

The
Conversion of
Mr. Krumbach

Oct. 2

Leo Rosten
Apt. 39-A
Vesuvius Towers
644 E. 68 St.
New York, N.Y. 10021

Dear Pal—

This is strictly on the Q.T.!! Between you
and me. Not to be even let on to in any way in any
missives you might be sending Flo, or vice-versa.
The reason is—it is about her own Old Man.

Well, 3-4 months ago Mr. Krumbach (Flos
Dad) who is close to 70 (from the other direction
ha, ha) and has been a widow for 6 years since his
wife past on, begins to look pretty tired and wore
out. He complanes about his back, hes not sleeping
good, his 2 eyes are wore out from his glasses (which
he changed with no effect)! hes losing his ap-
pettite, teeth, old pals, hes snapping at every
body and etc. and etc.

Flo kept telling the old man to re-tire, or
take it more easy and not work so hard, or even take
up fishing in nearby Lake Michigan, or play Golf
or some other healthfull hobby plus exercise.

But Mr. K. is not the type to do any of these

wise things, as he is a demon for work, work, work
who preaches to 1 and all: "Retirement has killed
more men than booze" or "If you keep your sholders
to the wheel, you will strenthen your back" and
somtimes even "I want to die with my boots on!"
(which gives me a hee-haw on account he never wore
a pair of boots in his life and thinks a "spur" is
what you have on the moment.)

So Flo goes off on a new tac, and she says
"Daddy, darling, why not go to 1 of them Hi-Brow
Seminnars for Execs. out in Asperin, Colo?"
And she tells him what a wonderfull experience it
was for Mr. Carmichael, who is the big Cadillac
distributor in these parts (his advertising is what
hooks people: "Buy Your Car from Carmichael!")

Flo is right on the ball there, because Mr.
Carmichael was the biggest sour-puss in Euphoria—
before he came back from an Asperin Round Table on
"U.S. Policy in the Far East". Now he is full of beans
and vinegar and with a whole new outlook on Life.
(Even without the Far East, which he is against.)

Well, Mr. Krumbach was sort of impressed
by that (knowing of Mr. Carmichaels record as a
rich millionaire). And to all our surprise, he
(Mr. K.) says "O.K. I will take a crack at it. What
do I have to loose?"

Which he does. In August (2 mos ago).

The old poop flys out to Colo.—and the Hi-
Brow Group he gets into is on "Freedom"—which
in spite of its title isnt a drag but contains some
peppy topics (like Minoritys, Civilian Liberties
and Women's Lib to top it all of.)

Me and Flo can hardly wait to see the Old
Mans effect, on account of his phone calls to us
Long Distance (which he does every night he is out
of town, sos he can talk googy-talk to his pet grand-

child, our Hortense ("Baby"). The old geezer
sounds like he is becoming a re-juveniled man. But
seeing is beleiving more than hearing, right?

So Mr. Krumbach returns. And Leo, you would
never beleive the diff. it has made in the old man
(in every way except Minority Rights or Civilian
Liberty.) It was Flos idea about her old man going
to those up-lifting discussions so as to "broaden
his horizon"—but she did not dream how broad-
minded he would become!

Now hold your hat, Buster Brown. 5 days after
Mr. K. has returned from his elevating condition
in the Rockys, a woman baring the name of Mrs.
Imogene Adjepouf breezes into Chicago and checks
in at the Sherman Hotel. And before you can say
"Bin-go!" she and the Old Man are having drinks
and dineing out and taking in all the night-spots
and floor-shows and doing the Ha-cha-cha like it is
1 week before Doom-day and they better live-it-up
whilst they can!

We hear all about this from Cora and Vern
Corrigan who as Frug and Monkey dance champs of our
country club practicly haunt all the Jet joints
in a 20-mile radios. And Flo is floored (to t it
mildily)! She gets right on the talk-line to her dear
Dad and asks him "Whats all this I hear about you
and some "fem fatal" from out-of-town?"

The Old Coot pores on the soft soap and tells
Flo (in a tone like a funeral director) that thats
the troubel with the world today—a man cant even
have 1 quiet dinner with an old friend who happens
to be of the female sex without a lot of yakking evil-
minds making a big stoosh about that.

"Who, pray, is this old friend?" shrewds
Flo.

"Her name is Mrs. Imogene Adjepouf (which

Mr. K. has to spell out, natch, its being a real
cross-word stopper, and that is how I come to get it
right) and she is a very refined widow who lives out
in near Denver, Colo. and took part in our bull-
sessions on Freedom—where we both hit if off like
2 twins in 3 shakes of a lams tail!"

"Perhaps Hermie and I should have the
pleasure of making her aquaintance" hints Flo.

"You are cooking with gas" the old man
chuckels.

So that very eve Mr. K. brings Mrs. A. over
to our home for a drink. He does not call her Mrs.
Adjepouf—but by her nick-name of "Eppie". And
she does not call him "Mr. Krumbach" but "you"
or even "Yoo-hoo" which sure means something,
right?

From my own instant observation, this dame
and the Old Crock being on the same wave-length
in Asperin had nothing to do with "egghead"
palaver about Freedom for Civillians but more to do
with Freedom in the Hay (if you know what I mean.)

Why do I say this? I will tell you why, Leo,
because actions speak louder then gossip.

In the 1st place, this "Eppie" Adjepouf
looks like a swinger—a Blond sex-pot, who in spite
of her age (at least 45) has a bilt or shape right
out of Playboy! One of Gods master-pieces (ha ha!)
In the 2d place, she is wearing a "frock" that fits
her like it is made out of Saran Rap. In the 3d spot,
Mr. K. is wearing new blinkers—not for reading
but in tribute to her avocados, which are worth it.
And in the # 4 slot, the Old Man and "Eppie" are
casting mushy goo-goo looks at each other and grinning like apes and her patting him on the hand or he
her on the can like 2 love-birds—as I implied in
the 1st place.

Well, I did not want to upset Flo with even
1 remark about such a moral mish-mosh regarding
her own Father, so I keep my trap shut. But Flo is
no dum-dum. She has eyes in back of her beano and a
7th sense about whats cooking in the "hot pants"
dept. (and I do not mean the garb of that denomina-
tion!)

So Mr. K. and "Eppie" parch their thirst
with potent cocktails and then head for "The Go-
Go Club" on the hi-way near Euphoria.

And our front-door chimes have hardly
stopped before Flo gives me the beady fish-eye as she
meditates out aloud "Sweet-heart, what was your
honest impression of Mrs. Imogene Adjepouf?"

"Well" I reply (seeing "Caution—Curves
Ahead") "she is a somewhat nifty specimen of her
age."

"I think she has had a face job" Flo
offers.

"I hardly noticed" I bunt.

"She belts down Martinis like her stomach
has a sponge lining" observes Flo.

"She was probly nervous her 1st time meeting you" I offer.

"I think she is a fast number!" glares
Flo.

"Your Dad has a new approach to the 50-
yard dash" I utter.

"She is a Bleach Blond" Flo murmurs in a
way that I can practicly hear the chip on her sholder.

"No kidden?!" I pretend.

"How old—just for fun—would you surmise
her to be?" caroons Flo.

"I figure her to be 75" I lie. "Give or
take 10 days."

"I think she is trying to throw her hooks into Daddy!" blurts out Flo.

"Maybe he is trying to pop his gum or gums at her" I smile.

"This is no joking matter!" Flo retorts. "I never in my whole life saw Daddy so icky in re a female—before or since Mother past on."

"It has done wonders for his looks, spirit, enerjy and point of view" I conclude.

Flo is word-less for 1 or 2 minuets, then asks me, like a cat sizing up a mouse "By the way, Herm love, how has Daddy been acting—down at the office?"

Man, I sure had to button a lip or 2 before replying to that, Leo! On account of the way Mr. K. is acting is like he is trying to beat Spencer Tracey for the lead in "Dr. Jekyl and Mr. Hide"—a real darb of a movie, if you remember the story.

Take his Sec. The old man has had the same old Sec. for ¼ of a century even before I went to work there, an old maid by the name of Hope Virginia Macintosh, who we all call (amongst each other) "Hopeless Virgin" Macintosh. She is a mean old bag—but very hard-working and real loyal to Mr. K. and the Co.

So what happens? Right after Mr. K. comes back from his magic conversion center in Colo. he tells Miss Macintosh he wants to reward her for all her years of service—with a free trip (all her expenses paid) of 41 days on a cruize from N.Y. all thru the Meditteranean with stop-overs in ports like Madrid, Gilbraltar, Tangerine, Sicily, Naple, Venus and etc.

The Hopeless Virgin was just flabbergassted (as who was not?)! She crys "O Mr. Krumbach I have allways dreamed of travel to exotical places, but my work here—well, I do not want to leave this job!"

The Old Fox doesnt bat 1 eye before re-smiling "Miss Macintosh you do not know what is for your own good. . . . There is a longer excursion—which takes in romantic Istanbull and the Isle of Roads."

Miss M. blubbers she did not dream Mr. K. thought so much about her—still, what about her job? "Will I still have it upon returning from the Sunny Medit?" (She is not so rum-dum after all when smelling a rat in the haystack of gold.)

Mr. K. gives her his open-skull smile, and finagels "Miss Macintosh this job is in no peril. It will go on. . . . So when you return from your glorius trip give me a buzz—and we will see."

"I dont want to leave this post" the sus-pitious crow hints "or lose it!"

"Dear Miss Macintosh" that old S.O.B. solemly caroons "you are a meer 2 years from re-tirement, and considering how hard you have worked it is equal to your allready being 65 instead of 63, so you will start to get all your re-tirement bene-fits. . . O do not look so sad, Miss Macintosh! This cruize will give you a whole new Lease on Life, just mark up my words—"

"I dont want to be put out to pasture!" protests Miss M.

"Well said!" exclaims Mr. K. "which is why I thought up an ocean trip. There is not 1 single pasture between N.Y. and the Asores."

"But when I return" the "H.V." persists in a way no one never dreamed that that slave type would "will I still be your—"

"Consultant!" hollers Mr. K. "I will buzz you 20-30 times a week. I will not make 1 impor-

tant decision regarding Cinderella without the
benefit of your in-valuabel Experience and Judge-
ment. That is why I want you to get away from all the
hum-and-drum burdens, Miss Macintosh. To open up
all your scopes, so when you re-turn you will not be
chained to that desk outside of my door but will be
able to think up new Ideas, and tred new trails away
from this office alltogether! In fact, now that I
realise how you feel, there is a 58-day trip in the
other direction, leaving L.A. for Hawaai and taking
in those wonderfull South Sea places like Honolulul,
Tahite, and parts of Polinesia where they shot
"Mutiny on the Bounty"."

     To make a long story short, Leo, Miss Hope
V. Mackintosh is now somewheres East of Suez. And
who is the Old Mans Personal Sec? You win the cigar,
Mac. Mrs. "Eppie" Adjepouf!!!

     Ce-ripes, how a matured man can change over-
night. The Old Goat is carrying on like he has hypod
up his motor thru a set of monkey glans. He pats that
broad Eppies sholder in "approval" if she puts
a sheet of paper in the typewriter the right way!
(He pats her elsewheres when she puts the sheet in
the wrong way, as far as that goes.)

     So there it is, pal.

     My problem is—Leo, do I level with Flo??
She threw a fit of temper-transom when she heard
that Miss Macintosh is sailing across the Pacifics
wild blue yonder while Mrs. Imogene Adjepouf is in
her Dads office!

     But the Old Fox soothd Flo with some cock-
amamy jazz about "Eppie" is meerly "filling in"
as a big "favor" to 1 and all until Miss Macintosh
"returns" from her educational journeys. But I
know that is doubble-talk, as the Old Geezer has
told me he has another excursion lined up for Miss

M. the minute her ship returns to L.A.! "I want
her to look into the market for laminated shims in
India" he grins me, like I was born yesterday "and
possibly in Austrialia."

I figure there are enough faraway places on
the map for him to keep the Hopeless Virgin out of
his hair until Social Security sets in. Which, if
you ask me, is the Old Coots Game Plan.

Leo, its only a matter of time before Flo
finds all this out! So should I brake the hole of the
news cold to her now, or wait and dish it out a little
at a time?

Your buddy,

"Herm"

P.S. For G---sake don't even drop 1 word about this
to Flo if she writes you! Or v.v.!!! I will get in
terribel Duch—and be up the creek, with no paddel
what-so-ever to talk my way out of spilling all this
inside stuff to a total stranger.

```
RFXO-934-URG.-
EUPHORIA ILL 47689-- Oct. 11 - 12:45 P.M. JFX 37N
RUSH


LEO ROSTEN
644 E. 68 STREET
NEW YORK CITY 10022

URGENT STOP FORGET MY LAST LETTER STOP DO NOT ANSWER
IN ANY WAY OR EVEN HINT THAT I EVER WROTE A PEEP
ABOUT A CERTAIN OLD MAN AND HIS COLORADO CRUSH STOP
MISTER KRUMBACH AND EPPIE HAVE ELOPED STOP LAST
NIGHT STOP AFTER MISTER K RECEIVED A TELEGRAM FROM
MISS MACINTOSH FROM HAWAII SAYING SHE IS FLYING
BACK FROM THERE WITHOUT GOING ONE PORT FARTHER ON
THAT 53-DAY CRUISE STOP I THINK FLO SECRETLY CABLED
MISS MACINTOSH AND PUT HER UP TO THIS STOP SO HER
FATHER NAILED FLO WITH HIS TRUMP CARD STOP SO WIPE
OUT OF YOUR MIND EVERYTHING I WROTE ABOUT A CERTAIN
MATTER AND BURN THE LETTER OR I WILL GET IN TERRIBLE
TROUBLE WITH HIM AND THE BRIDE AND FLO ETCETERA STOP
DO NOT EVEN ANSWER THIS WIRE STOP

                              HERM K
```

LEO ROSTEN
Apt. 39-A
644 E. 68 St.
New York, N.Y. 10021

Oct. 13

Dear Flo:

We are having dandy weather in Manhattan.
The temperature is in the 70s and the humidity is
low so therefore the weather is very pleasant to
one and all.

What a fine time of year this is, Flo—when
the weather is nice. The trees are in full leaf in
Central Park, and many a bird is singing its head
off (unlike me, who never did sing. Right, Herm?)

I just thought I would drop you a note because
I have not heard a peep from either of you in ages!
That made me wonder why I have not heard from either
of you in so long. Have you two been too busy, or
vice-versa?

How are things out in Euphoria? I hope you
are both in good health—and happy spirits. And
how are the kids doing at Shimmel?

I am just sort of curious to hear what (if
anything, of course) is new—concerning any of
your large and interesting family, new friends,
unusual events, etc. I guess you might say that
I pine for news. Any news.

Your lonely friend,

Leo

Mrs. Herman P. Klitcher
201 Placebo Park
Euphoria, Ill. 60035

Oct. 15

Mr. Leo Rosten
Apt. 39-A
Vesuvius Towers
644 E. 68 St.
New York, N.Y. 10021

<u>Cher, Cher Ami</u> Leo:

How sweet of you to write that <u>billet</u> and
ask about all of we friends (and fans!) of yours.
You must be very lonely—as I know any true <u>artiste</u>
must, from time to time. That is the fate of the
creative type.

<u>Alors,</u> all is quiet on the western front
(I <u>loved</u> Lew Ayers as the soldier in that memmorable
example of cinema art!) Hermie is fine, tho working
like two beavers, as is his nature. Penelope (the
"Bubbles" you know) is going to be in the Drama
Club's <u>Potpourri Night,</u> where she will play one of
the ungratefull daughters in <u>King Leer.</u>

Alvin is making a model-plane out of light
Baltic wood and strong, very "smelly" glue.
(Thank <u>God</u> he is not "sniffing" it, if you know
what I mean, as was the case of a certain teen-ager
in our shocked community.)

Mildred's pidgeons are cooing and billing

more than ever in their darling home over our garage
—and this year we have not had a scare about skin
splotches or mangey feathers, as we did a few sea-
sons back.

Hortense (forever our "Baby") is painting
a huge "collage" in our game room—of the Chi.
and Northwest R.R. train's various station-stops
between downtown Wabash Avenue all the way up here
through Skokie and Highland Park. A very interesting
work of art, _je croix,_ as it consists of painted
colors plus matches, pieces of calendars, burlap
and an egg carton which shows a striking resemblance
to the Chicago sky-line at dusk (as seen from the
rear of the train).

As for _moi,_ I am going right on—with family
and communal duties, now and then at the Seeds and
Shrub Society and our weekly girls get-together
for Cannasta.

Tiens! That takes care of every Klitcher,
and that is _all_ the news!

Now, what about you? What new master-work
are you cooking up? Will it be in the comic line
or other-wise?

We keep watching for your name (or _nom de
plume_) on the Late Show and the Late Late Show, but
have missed it for some time. Don't you just _hate_
TV, sometimes?

Waiting to hear from you about recent and
up-coming exploits, we all remain

Votre ami

Florence ("Flo") K.

P.S. O, I just remembered one thing. I don't suppose
Hermie ever had the chance to tell you. My father

has married! Of course, we have all been expecting
this for many moons as the lucky lady is an old
friend of the family's (I mean my father's family).
Altho we have not seen much of her in recent years,
since she has lived in a beautiful mountain <u>chalet</u>
in Colorado, we have all heard my father talk about
her for <u>years</u>—and with true, deep respect.

So I have a new friend as well as new "step-"
mother. Her name before becoming Mrs. Lionel F.
Krumbach was Imogene Adjepouf—a dissentent from
a famous Hungarian family of nobles. It is a real
<u>coup de grace</u> for us. For it is not every day an
Adjepouf comes to Euphoria!!

The bride is close to Daddy's age, tho a
bit younger, which is a good thing, in some ways.
<u>N'est ce pas?</u> She is attractive (for a widow of
those years) tho some people might think she is
too "sophisticated"—which is due to her refined
upbringing and her training in music, when she
studied to be an opera <u>divan</u> in her youth (I think).
<u>All of us</u> think she is very refined, which is more
important.

We were <u>dying</u> to have the wedding in our
own home—but Daddy and "Eppie" (as Imogene is
called) would not <u>hear</u> of our putting ourselfs out
in that way. So they just slipt away for the quiet
exchange of martial vows.

I want Hermie to add his few words to these
sentiments. Here he comes.

"Flo"

P.P.S. Hi, pal, this is Herm coming in—to confirm
every word Flo has told you so far! I sure was let

down not to have the wedding between Flos dad and
Mrs. Adjepouf in our own home here. But him and his
"Bride-to-be" were absolutly decided against
a show-off type affair. So as Flo has told, they did
the deed fast, and without an excess of publicity.

Flo and me are real fond of our new "mother",
who is very refined and has also made a hit with our
4 offsprings!

So thats about the only news from the
Klitcher clan. So Long, pal—and thanks for everything in true pal-ship.

Your old buddy,

"Herm"

The Inside Dope
on
Noah's Ark

Nov. 12

Leo Rosten
Apt. 39-A
Vesuvius Towers
644 E. 68 St.
New York, N.Y. 10021

Dear Leo:

Well, April Showers are sure driving us
batty (in Nov.)! You never in your whole <u>life</u> saw
such rains or a huricane as we have enjoyed the
passed 4 days, and no releif in sight! Every human
or even beast in Euphoria is in a lousy mood after
6-½"of rain, pore, drip, rain, pore, rain, pore,
rain, rain, rain, rain! And when it doesnt rain it
drivels.

Flo even gloomed "Maybe we are in for
another 30-day Flood like the one in the Bible!"

My heart sure sank, so I came right back
at her "That is just a cock-and-bull myth with no
foundation in fact!"

"You mean you do not beleive in <u>Noah and
the Arc?!</u>" snapped Flo.

"No I do not" I declare "And you wont find

a single well-educated man who beleives that after
Noah was swallowed by a Whale he took 2 of each type
animal (including moths, rhinos and even elephants)
on that little tub! How could any olden type boat
be big enough for a load like that?! Use your common
cents, sweet-heart! Noah did not even have real
tools, nails, screws, bolts, nuts, skillfull labor
and etc. Why that job would take 1,000 huge boats,
each 1 of them bigger than the Queen of Elizabeth!
And each boat would need U.S. Steel plus all Annap-
oliss shipyards."

  Well, that really burned Flo up, and she
blew her top. About me always looking at the nasty
or "synical" side of anything being discussed,
and allways dragging in so-call "facts" you
cant even have faith in them.

  "Well" I retort "you were the 1 that asked
me how I feel about the 30-day Flood in the Bible,
and all I did was answer I did not think Noah's Arc
was a real happening that took place!"

  "Then exactly what was it, wise guy?"
she snears.

  "Just an Old-Wives Tail! Like when your
corns hurt that means its going to rain. I supose
the Flood we are having right now in this area is
because of the number of old ladys whos bonions
are hurting!"

  Well, that made Flo blow a gasket and before
you know it we are having a slam-bang rubarb worse
than the type the Cubs and White Sox used to in the
good old days. So 1 harsh word leads to another and
the next thing I know Flo is threatening she will
call up the preacher in The Church of her Choice and
put it up to him—and any expert on Noah will blow
my position into a cooked hat! And she storms out
of the room we were in at the time.

Flo is sleeping in "Babys" room tonight (whilst Baby is staying over-night with "Jelly" (Jennifer) Tomish who lives down the street). Which is why I am sitting here all alone composing this appeal to you.

Leo, do you yourself trust that Noah and the Arc bit?!

Bible or no Bible, I say some things just dont make sense unless you use the brain God gave you to use—even when reading the Bible. Right? And in that case, Noah and his Arc are just an old-fashion fable, like cannibals crossing the Alps.

That is how I feel. Hoping you agree,

Your old class-mate

"Herm"

P.S. The rain is still coming down in buckets, like cats and ducks. Would you beleive it??

"H"

LEO ROSTEN
Theologian
1035 Divinity Drive
Heavenly Road
Uganda

Nov. 26

Herman P. Klitcher
210 Placebo Park
Euphoria, Illinois

Dear Herm:

I am ready to believe anything, even though
it has not rained for 46 days in a row here in pic-
turesque Uganda.

Your vivid description of your spat with
Flo provided me with much food for thought.

Do I take the story of Noah's Ark literally?
Frankly, Herm, no. Nor did Noah put much stock in
it. He might have crammed 30-40 animals into that
home-made craft, but not much more. The fact that
Noah got away at all, given his problems with the
gnus (Noah's gnus were not good gnus), is miracle
enough for me.

Herm, I think you and Flo have missed the
most interesting part of the whole story: Before
Noah loaded up, God appointed an angel to name each
pair of animals as they came up the gangplank. This
angel, whose name was Meyer, was stationed on the
poop-deck, from which he gave each animal couple a
long, searching look before he chose a name for them.

Take the yellow-coated Mongolian deer
with the enormous antlers. Meyer named them "Altai-
Wapiti." The other angels, who were jealous of
Meyer, were watching him like a whatever they called
a hawk before that name was allocated. And when
Meyer touched the shoulder of the male yellow-
coated deer with his sword, announcing, "I dub
thee 'Altai-Wapiti'!" the angels promptly protested: "But Meyer, why are you calling that
yellow-coated, enormous-antlered monstrosity
an 'Altai-Wapiti'?"

Meyer answered, "Because he _looks_ like
an Altai-Wapiti, that's why."

I do not believe this. I _admire_ it, Herm,
but cannot bring myself to believe it.

I do happen to know that Meyer named other
deer "Hello" and "Good-bye." That is the origin
of our custom of saying "Hello (or Good-bye), dear."

If you stop to think of it, Herm, one of the
really amazing things Man has done is to give different names to different things. This was not
easy. An ichthyologist for instance, can't just
dive down to a Blunt-Nosed Flounder, say, and ask:
"Excuse me, fish: I am taking a poll for the U.S.
Census Bureau. What is your name, please?"

Census Bureau fish-namers did try this
system at first, Herm, but they got fouled up something terrible, because the fish had all seen "To
Tell the Truth" (on cable TV). So every single fish
when asked, "What is your name, please?" gave the
same answer: "Glp."

The ichthyologists jumped to the conclusion
that all fish were named "Glp," but when they
fed this into a computer and asked for its opinion,
quick as a flash came the read-out: "No, No, No!"
Herm, when a computer answers "No, no, no!" in-

stead of just flipping its discs, you can be sure
something very important has happened in the world
of science.

The same thing happened to the zoologists,
who were assigned to name mammals. <u>Every single
specimen of a species, when interviewed, gave the
same name.</u> Every dog, for instance, said his name
was "Bark." Every cat said its name was "Meow,"
every cow, "Moo." And so on.

For a while, people went around calling
every dog "Bark," and no one minded; but when
men began to move out to the suburbs and called their
dogs in at night to give them their vitamin-enriched
chopped liver, any single call of "Here, Bark!
Here, Bark!" brought every dog in the neighborhood
to the caller's door. They came like lemmings, and
many died of overeating.

Things couldn't go on this way, so dog-
ologists decided to name each breed separately, once
and for all. I regret to say that they gave many a
dog a bad name. Take "Schnauzer." Anyone knows
that if you call a sensitive dog "Schnauzer,"
he will develop postnasal drip. Or take "Afghan."
A dog named "Afghan" is pretty sure to break out
in patches. The fact that each patch is a different
color only adds to the poor dogs' confusion; that
is why there are more schizophrenics among Afghans
than among any leading brand in the country.

I hope this gives you all the information
you need to answer Flo with authority.

In whose room is she sleeping these nights?

Your buddy,

Leo

P.S. Remember how, at Crane Tech, we used to sing
"It ain't gonna rain Noah more, Noah more"? They
don't get off puns like that anymoah.

P.P.S. What ever happened to Miss Macintosh?

**From the Desk of
Herman P. Klitcher**

Dec. 1

Dear Leo—

     The "Hopeless Virgin" is cleaning up
a bundel—as Ship Steno on the S.S. Coronaria!
(They do those Millionair-Only-Around-the-World-
Tours.)
     Man, how Fate turns things inside out!
The S.S. Coronaria had like 170 applications for
the job—and why did Miss Hope V. Macintosh win out?
On account they tested all the hopefulls for sea-
sickness, and she was the only 1 they couldnt even
get woozy. That old bat wouldnt even throw up castro
oil or kidneys a la mode.
     No one at Cinderella ever dreamed Miss
Macintosh had such a talent, as she allways used
to eat her lunch out of a paper bag.

"Herm"

P.S. It only goes to show how true is that old saying
"Every dog has her day."

Flying Saucers

HORTENSE KLITCHER

Dec. 10

Dear Mr. R—

   Being so helpfull to the Klitchers about
many various questions, I have one that is driving
me bananas! In our place of abode we argue about
it and get nowheres. That is: about Flying Saucers.
   What is your frank opinion? Should we accept
them??
   With oodles of thank yous,

            Your friend in need,

            Hortense Klitcher

LEO ROSTEN
Astrophysicist
97 Milky Way
Galaxy
Texas

Dec. 14

Dear Hortense:

    Flying saucers are just an optical con-
clusion. I would not accept one, even as a gift.
They are extremely unstable and when they start
zooming around they can knock out all the windows
in a person's place of abode.

Your pal,

— L. R.

HORTENSE KLITCHER

Dec. 17

Dear Mr. R—

    You are something else again! (Aren't you?)
The living end.

    Your reply is a gasser, tho far away from
the point. Miss Raskolnikov once said, "Some
people will do anything for a pun!" (No need to
mention names!!!)

    Why don't you just come out of the rain?!

              Your friend (?)

              Hortense

HOT CROSS PUNS
from
LEO LYON

Dec. 20

Dear Hortense—

    I love the rain (as did Queen Victoria).
In fact, my favorite verse is:
    "The goodly rain doth fall
    Upon the just and unjust fellow,
    But mostly on the just
    Because
    The unjust stole the just's um-
        brella."

                  Yours

            Edgar Allen Poem

HORTENSE KLITCHER

Dec. 22

Dear Mr. R—

Sticks and stones may break my bones but
words will never hurt me!
Are you for <u>real?!</u>

Hortense

<u>EPITAPHS</u>
from
<u>LEO ROSTEN</u>

Dec. 24

Dear Hortense—

        Really! I realize you have never seen me
reel. You would, were we realated.

                              Yours,
                    Roster Real Estate, Inc.

Merry Christmas.

The Toughest
Brain-Teaser
in the World

HERMAN P. KLITCHER
210 Placebo Park
Euphoria, Ill. 60035

Jan. 3

Leo Rosten
Vesuvius Towers
644 E. 68 St.
New York, N.Y. 10021

Dear Leo—

Happy New Year, I hope. Its been a long time
since I have not heard a peep out of you. Are you
O.K. in all respects as of yore?

Well, pal, heres a pip! This whole passed
week Flo keeps throwing me a very interesting but
<u>hard</u> Brain-Teaser—which I am going nuts trying
to figure it out! Flo refuses to tell me the answer
—which she claims she knows (she admits she did
not work it out for herself but got it from Caprice
Slotnick). Caprice is her best friend, but a real
trouble-maker with who she spends <u>hours</u> batten
her gums in girly-girly gossip—mostly about
"Frenchy" Lastfogel.

To get back to the Riddel (Brain-Twister.)
I have put in 4-5 whole hours on it—and take it from
me, buddy, I am stumped! But <u>cold.</u> Here is how Flo
told me the G-- d-- thing—

"Jack, who is a piano-
tuner, is moving to Buffalo. He
is two years older than Dolores.
Dolores is one inch shorter than
her brother Max, whose nick-name
is "Giraffe." But Max's brother
is named Ajax, and his last name
is not relevent . . . Okay: What
is the conductor's name?"
Leo, don't tell theres no fly in that there ointment!

Flo gooses me every night I come home
"Okay, Brain, have you figured it out as yet??
You always say Men are smarter than Females any
time. So go ahead. Show me. What is the name of the
conducter???"

And do I feel like a dummy! Every time, pal.

So what do I do? Leo, I <u>pretend</u> I have figured out the answer—but do not intend to give her
the satisfaction of telling it!

So she keeps needeling me.

So I say "I will reveal the answer in my
own sweet time!"

I do not think Flo beleives me, Leo. Because
whenever I say I am not going to give her the cheap
satisfactin she is after, she puts on her mockery
and coos "O.K. Lover, take your own sweet time
—and maybe by the time Xmas roles around I will
have the pleasure of telling your wrong solution
to all the girls at our Cannasta Club."

So—please help me out, Leo. The flack
is killing me! In the riddel (above) who the H---
is the conducter? Jack, Max, Ajax—or even Dolores?

Your old pal,

"Herm"

<u>Brain-Tease Solver</u>
96 Maze Mews
Okenefee Swamp
Maine

                                        Jan. 12

Herman P. Klitcher
210 Placebo Park
Euphoria, Ill. 60035

Dear "Herm":

        You have come to the right man. Even when
I was in knee-pants I guessed the answer to that oldie:
        "What is black and white and red
                all over?"
        The answer is: "A newspaper"!
        You see, the catch is in the word "red,"
Herm. Hearing the word "red" traps you into
thinking it is a color, like black or white. But
once you realize that "red" is also the way "read"
(which is a verb and not a color) is pronounced, the
answer is obvious. Newspapers are "black and white"
in appearance, but they are read ("red") all
over!! That is why "A newspaper" is the correct answer.
        The same is true of Flo's brain-teaser.
If you are on the alert to <u>each clue,</u> Herm, taking
one at a time, and don't let yourself be bamboozled
by the deliberately tricky way in which the puzzle
is formulated, the answer is a cinch. Take it step
by step:

1) "Jack, who is a piano-tuner, is moving to Buffalo."

That means he does not live there now. Right? Therefore he is not Buffalo Bill. (The information that Jack is a piano-tuner just tries to throw you off the track.)

2) "Jack is two years older than Dolores."

That means he is not younger than Dolores, so they are probably going around together.

3) "Dolores is only one inch shorter than her brother Max."

Well, since Max is very tall (only very tall men are nick-named "Giraffe"), Dolores should go out for volley-ball. Any girls' volleyball squad will welcome a tall girl. (Boys' volleyball teams are different; they like to play with short girls, too.)

4) "Max's brother is named Ajax."

This means that Ajax is Dolores' brother, too, because she is Max's sister—therefore she is Ajax's sister too. (I'll bet that point slipped past you.)

5) "Ajax's last name is not relevant."

Well, if Ajax's last name is not "Relevant," then neither is Max's or Dolores's! (Siblings always have the same last name. Right?)

6) Ergo:

If neither Max, Ajax nor Dolores is named Relevant, then their last name is Toscanini, which is a perfect name for a conductor.

That leaves only one point to be cleared up, Herm: Who is "Frenchy" Lastfogel?

Your old pal,

Leo

P.S. Can't you knock off Caprice Slotnick, who told Flo that brain-teaser? In our day in old Chi. you could get a tomato like that bumped off for 50 or 60 bucks. I know inflation has hit Euphoria, but if I were in your place I would not consider 500 G's too high to get such a yenta off my back.

— L

From the Desk of Herman P. Klitcher

Jan. 20

Dear Leo:

Criminy, Leo, you have to be kidding! Can't
you ever be serious?? I have a real problem and you
make with the cock-eye jokes instead of answers a
person could get very angry with!!
"Frenchy" Lastfogel has nothing what-
so-ever to do with the riddel! She is just the bubbel-
head who Flo and Caprice Slotnick rake over their
coal. (She is not called "Frenchy" for nothing.
If you know what I mean.)
Flo still keeps needeling me to "Put up
or shut up!!" (about the Brain-Teaser in re Jack,
Buffalo, Max, etc.) What should I tell her???

Desperetely,

"Herm"

Jan. 25

Dear Desk of Herman P. Klitcher:

      Tell Flo that Caprice Slotnik is a bird-
brain who screwed-up the clues in the brain-teaser
so badly that no one can guess the answer. (That
will kill two birds with the same stone.) If you
smile pityingly while saying this, Flo will go
into a panic and get right back to Caprice. Since
women rarely know how to recite a riddle correctly,
Flo and Caprice will soon be snapping at each other
like sharks. They may even stop talking to one
another.
      I know of a case where a pair of devoted
sisters, Mia and Culpa Fledermaus, had such a vio-
lent argument about an old family recipe for root
beer that they appealed to their mother, who called
both of them dummies. As a result, all three have
not uttered another word to one other since 1963.
You may be just as lucky.

Your pal,

Desk of Leo Rosten

P.S. If Caprice asks Flo, "Okay, Smarty Pants, what
is the right way to relate that brain-teaser?"
tell Flo to reply that she knows the correct way,

but won't give Caprice the satisfaction of pro-
viding the right answer until she (Caprice) comes.
up with the right question. (Ha, ha.)

From the Desk of
Herman P. Klitcher

Jan. 29

Dear Leo:

You are great! Just great!

I did what you said—and man, did Flo turn
on the heat! She phoned Caprice Slotnick right away,
and that scrambeld-egg got all flustered and she
alibid all over the joint and then hollered not to
blame <u>her</u> if the Brain-Teaser was all loused up because thats the way she heard it from—none other
than "Frenchy" Lastfogel!!

So Flo buzzed <u>"Frenchy"</u>—and boy, did you
ever call the shot on that! Inside of a minuet those
2 broads are snapping at each other like those fish
in Brazil who eat human flesh but cant <u>stand</u> each
other. Flo accused "Frenchy" of never getting <u>any-
thing</u> right, and "Frenchy" said "Like what for
example?" and Flo came right back at her with what
caused all the trouble between Cornelia Kolatsch
and Flo—because "Frenchy" said that Cornelia was
showing too much of her boobies at parties, in order
to excite other happily married men. And Flo agreed.
So Cornelia said that if thats the way Flo feels she
will never step foot in our house again!! Which is
hunky-dorey with me. Not because I do not enjoy the
way "Corny" Kolatsch is stacked (man, she is as
<u>zaftig</u> as May West in her prime of life) but on

account I cant stand her creep of a mate—Merwyn
B. Kolatsch, a double for Boris Karloff if you ever
saw one, the biggest boar in Euphoria.

Thanks a million, pal! You are a genius!!

Your buddy,

"Herm"

P.S. What is the right way of putting that Brain-
Teaser? I have to know, Leo, as now Flo is nagging
me so she can tell it correct to Caprice and have
Caprice give "Frenchy" Lastfogel her just de-
serts.

LEO ROSTEN
President
<u>Anagrams, Inc.</u>
330 Puzzle Gulch
Sadism
Oklahoma

Feb. 2

Herman P. Klitcher
210 Placebo Park
Euphoria, Ill. 60035

Dear Herm:

The correct way to put the brain-twister
is this:
Jack is moving his buffaloes to
be near a cowboy named Bill. Bill is four
years older than his aunt, Brunnhilde.
Since he (Jack) is 2" shorter than Max,
who drives a kayak, the last name of Dolores
is not relevant—but Shultz. So:
What is the name of the character
(not "conductor") Humphrey Bogart played
in "Casablanca"?

Do you see what a difference this way of
putting it makes?

Your ever-ready friend,

Leo

P.S. The answer is: "Rick." That is the name of
the character Bogie played in "Casablanca".
     I hope your troubles are now over.

— ℒ

HERMAN P. KLITCHER
210 Placebo Park
Euphoria, Ill. 60035

Feb. 6

Dear Leo—

Like H--- my troubles are all over! Stop
making up those Yo-Yo addressess and stick to the
points!

All that Casablanca crapola is a <u>red her-
ring,</u> if you ask me. Bogie has <u>nothing to do</u> with
Jack, Max, Dolores. Plus you have even dropped out
"Ajax" alltogether. (<u>I</u> figure him to be the key
to the whole thing, but dont know why.)

Anyways, Flo has really wised up to me just
<u>pretending</u> I know the answer. She is now giving
me the needle in spades—and at public parties and
barbecues!

I am at my wits ends and ready to say
"O.K. O.K. I give up!" and throw in the towel! What
should I do?

Your pal,

"Herm"

192

LEO ROSTEN
President
<u>Friendship, Inc.</u>
64 Quaker Peak
Philadelphia,
Tennessee

Feb. 9

Dear "Herm":

    Don't throw in the towel. Victory is star-
ing you right in the face.

Your pal,

Leo

HERMAN P. KLITCHER
210 Placebo Park
Euphoria, Ill. 60035

Feb. 12
(Lincolns Birthday)

Leo Rosten
Apt. 39-A
Vesuvius Towers
644 E. 68 St.
New York, N.Y. 10021

Dear Leo:

    God d--- it! <u>What</u> victory is stareing me
in <u>what</u> face (or anywhere else)?
    The only way I can get off of Flos hook is
to give her the right question and answer to that
friggin Brain Twister!!
    I have come to the unpleasantish conclusion
that I bet <u>you</u> are faking and dont know the answer
either!!

                 Disgusted,

                 "Herm"

LEO ROSTEN
Honesty Personified, Inc.
True Blue Lane
Verity
Vermont

Feb. 22
(Washington's Birthday)

Herman P. Klitcher
210 Placebo Park
Euphoria, Ill. 60035

Dear "Herm":

    Don't jump to conclusions.

                              Yours,

                              Leo

**From the Desk of
Herman P. Klitcher**

Dear Leo:

    Whos "jumping" to a conclusion?! I have
been trying for <u>weeks</u> to get the right way out of
you to put that Brain-Twister—and the right answer
to it as well!

    Stop all this futzing around, and get off
your Yo-Yo! For once and all—Do you or dont you
know the right answer?!!

From the
Desk
of
Leo Rosten

Dear Desk:

Yes.

Leo

**From the Desk of
Herman P. Klitcher**

Dear Leo—
 O.K., Mac! What is it??

"Herm"

LEO ROSTEN
President
Patience in All Things, Inc.
St. Frances of Assisi Lane
Puxatawney
Sicily

Herman P. Klitcher
210 Placebo Park
Euphoria, Illinois 60035

Dear Herm:

The answer to the brain-teaser is

Yours,

Leo

**From the Desk of
Herman P. Klitcher**

Dear Leo—

   I do not regard that as even funny!!

                              "Herm"

From the
<u>Desk</u>
of
<u>LEO ROSTEN</u>

Dear Herm:

      Neither do I.

Leo

P.S. To help you recover prestige, ask this one of
Flo, Caprice and "Frenchy":

      A big Indian and a little Indian
      are walking through the woods. The little
      Indian is the big Indian's son, but the
      big Indian is not the little Indian's
      father!

      Explain.

— L

Cinderella LAMINATED SHIMS
83 Wacker Drive
Chicago, Illinois 60612

March 2

Leo Rosten
Apt. 39-A
Vesuvius Towers
644 E. 68 St.
New York, N.Y. 10021

Dear Leo:

Brother, you are really something!! Your
brain-teaser about the 2 Indians (walking thru
the woods) was the hi-light of our conversing at
Helmut and "Vicky" Tushs house at the party they
threw last Sat. night. They had a real turnout (24!).
So around 9 P.M. I told them your riddel.

Man, it sure started all tongs wagging!
It must of been 2 A.M. before we broke up—and no
1 got the answer!! Here are the shots in the dark
by our varies efforts in that direction:

1) The big Indian is the little Indian's
father-in-law! (Except we all agreed that isnt
right, on account a little Indian is probly to young
to have married a squaw.)

2) In the tribe these two Redskins belong
to, the Chief is all of the kids father—so no Brave
is allowed to be called Father by any kid except that
Chief! (Except no one at the Tushs party could

name such a tribe, so we voted to table that concept.)

3) The little Indian was <u>adopted</u> while still a pickaninny, so the big Indian is the little Indians <u>step</u>-father. (Except if that is the case, the little Indian would be a <u>step-son,</u> which is not mentioned, so that must be an iffy type answer, right?)

4) The big Indian is the little Indians <u>brother!</u> (That answer—by Monty O. Nayfish—created the big sensation! We all were ready to holler Bingo! until Flo (who sure has her head glud to her shoulders) reminded—"But the little Indian is the big Indians son, so how can the big Indian be the little Indians brother?! A brother cant be a son —and vise-versa! Boy, was Monty O. p----- off to have the rag pulled out from under him.)

So thats where we let it lay, Leo—with the gang begging me to get the real answer by phoning you on the spot, they were so hot for the solution. But I reminded them how it is 1 hour later in N.Y. then out in these parts—which I learned the hard way (the time I tried to get you on Long Distance) and every person agreed it was the wrong thing to do to wake somebody up at 3 A.M. your time. (Besides, I still dont have your homes unlisted number!)

Well, now it's up to you, pal. And I hope this isnt another 1 of your cockamamy jokeroos!! Answer fast.

If the little Indian is the big Indians son, and the big Indian (as you claim) is <u>not</u> the little Indian's father—then what the h--- is he?

Your old buddy

"Herm"

LEO ROSTEN
Doctor of Genealogy
Paleface Path
Sioux Falls
Ohio

Herman P. Klitcher
Cinderella Laminated Shims, Inc.
83 Wacker Drive
Chicago, Illinois 60612

Dear Herm:

      His mother.

                      Bravely yours,

                        Leo

P.S. I am sorry to learn Flo's head is glued to her
shoulders. If I were you, I would advise her to
undergo surgery. Her head should be on her neck.

"Pidge"
Writes My
Autobiography

Cinderella LAMINATED SHIMS
83 Wacker Drive
Chicago, Illinois 60612

April 5

Leo Rosten
Apt. 39-A
Vesuvius Towers
644 East 68 St.
New York, N.Y. 10021

Dear Leo:

Great news!! And I know you will get just as
pepped up about it as my wife Flo and me when the news
came to us.

Last night our Mildred, age 15 (who as you
know every one calls "Pidge"—on account of she
raises them in a coot on top of our garage) related
to me and her mother Flo that Miss Ickelheimer, who
teaches Junior English at Shimmel High, has given
that class their this-terms Term Paper topic, which
is—

"Write a 500-words Autobiography
of the American Author, living or dead, who
you admire the most."

And "Pidge" chose you!!!

Wow, Leo! Isn't that <u>something?!</u> Who would
of ever dreamed back in our own H.S. days at Crane
Tech that 1 of my own flash-and-blood would be
writing up a famous man who it happens was her own

Daddys school chum maybe ¼ of a century ago?! If
that isnt Fate I sure would like to know what is?!

So will you just answer Pidges questions—
which I enclose? So she can have real first-hand
info. and not meer gossip—about things like your own
psycology, ways of life, Religion, personal hobbys,
and etc.

Pidge wanted to write to you her-self, but
frankly "the cat has her tong" when it comes to
writing. (Even when Flo tells her she has to write
a Thank You note about say a birthday present.) A
person who did not know her would think she (Pidge)
was having an apoleptic fit when the time comes for
her to pen a missive.

Well, Pidge begged me to write to you, but I
put my feet down and said she would have to write up
the list of questions her-self that she wants your
answers to—which I have put inside this envelope.
Pidge is so excited awaiting your answers that she
cant hardly keep her mind on other subjects, such as
Algebra, Gym, or History. That is not your fault,
of course, Leo, but I just want you to know how
excited she actualy is!

You will be the first living Author she ever
got a letter from! And I bet you 2-1 that when she
brings that epistle to school and displays it to Miss
Ickelheimer and all her chums, of who she has plenty,
being very popular (in the Drama Club she stole the
show by her acting in "The Merchant of Venus"),
she is also V.P. of the Shimmel High "Hobby Hole,"
and things like you answering her will go a long way
to building up her popularity in the eyes of her
fellow-students.

Well, I will now say Oh Revoir as Flo likes
to say.

Waiting to hear by return mail, because Pidges autobiog. of you has to be handed in by April 15!

Your old pal,

"Herm"

P.S. Her questions are in this envelope, in case you threw it away.

P.P.S. Excuse the typeing. I did not want to trust such a personal letter to my new Secretary, who is something for the birds! This morning she comes in at 11 o'clock (!) and when I said sternly "You should of been here at 10!" she bats her eye lashes (which are so heavy they give her round shoulders) and murmurs "Why? What happened?"

Ce-ripes, Leo, what a bus. man has to go thru these days!

(Enclosure)
10 Questions for Mr. Leon Rosten
by
Mildred Klitcher

1) Where were you actually born?
2) What occupation was your Father?
3) Did your mother influense you often?
4) What was your boyhood ambition?
5) Of all the books you wrote, which is your favorit?
6) What writing methods do you adopt when writing your master-pieces?

7) How do you get your easy, careless style? (Do you just dictate it off to a steno. that gives it such a breezy feeling?)

8) Do you use "pen-names" all the time (like Leonore Q. Ross for those H* Y* M* A* N K* A* P* L* A* N stories?) Give examples.

9) Do you have any hobbys or things you do in your free time (when not writing?)

10) What is the best way for a new author to break into a magazine?

11) Were you ever a War Hero? If not, explain.

Thanking you for your fine reply to me,

Yours truly,

Mildred Klitcher

age 15

(daughter of Herman and Florence P. Klitcher)

Author of Note
Lowly Chasm
Wyoming

April 14

Herman Klitcher
210 Placebo Park
Euphoria
Illinois

Dear "Herm":
        Wow! I certainly was excited by your news.
Even as a boy, I never dreamed I would be the class-
mate of a guy whose 15-year-old daughter wants to
write an autobiography of.
        I hope the answers which I enclose will
please Pidge as well as you and your wife Flo.

                        Your friend,

                        Leo

                Enclosure
                  from
                Leon Rosten

        Answers to Mildred ("Pidge") Klitcher

1)   "Where were you actually born?"

I was actually born in an abandoned rut near Coxsackie, N.Y.

2) "What occupation was your Father?"

My father was not an occupation, per se; he was preoccupied most of the time. He worked as a printer in charge of typographical errors for a paper in Alaska. (The motto of the paper was: "Yukon fool all of the people all of the time.") It was from my dad that I learned there's no place like Nome.

3) "Did your mother influence you often?"

Very often. She made pillowcases out of sandpaper. One of them was embroidered "Send a Salami To a Boy in the Army," and started me on my career as a writer.

4) "What was your boyhood ambition?"

To go into metallurgy. But when they found out I was allergic to metal, I began to make stilts for midgets.

5) "Of all the books you wrote which is your favorite?"

Hamlet.

6) "What method do you use in writing your master-pieces?"

For masterpieces, I write in long-hand, dividing the numerator by the divider. For minor pieces, I write about people under 21.

7) "How do you get your easy, careless style? Do you just dictate it off to a steno that gives it such a breezy feeling?"

I attribute my easy, careless style to the fact that my pen leaks. My "breezy" style, on the other hand (I have two), is what happens when I write out-of-doors.

8) "Do you employ 'pen-names' all the time . . .?"

I have used a "pen-name" ever since my son was stoned by his classmates.

Examples: I used George Eliot when writing "Silas Mariner," and James Sherman for "The Anti-Trust Laws."

9) "Do you have any special hobbys or things you do in your free time (when not writing)?"

I enjoy counting my knuckles, of which I have 58 on my hands and feet alone.

My hobby is tying garottes. Sometimes I stuff olives into nuts, instead of the other way around, as is usually done in fine food stores everywhere.

I also have an old collection of boomerangs, which I can't get rid of.

10) "What is the best way for a new writer to break into a magazine?"

The best way for anyone to break into a magazine is by using a chisel or Jimmy. The reason I recommend a chisel or Jimmy instead of a skeleton key, is that most skeletons will not let anyone else use their key.

11) "Where you ever a War Hero? If not, explain."

I do not like to boast about my war record. That is why my deeds as a Hero must remain incognito. I hope you will not tell this to anyone.

Your favorite author,

Leon Rosten

Age 34 (Son of Lassie).

Take the Quokka,
or the Delightful
Bandicoot

Cinderella LAMINATED SHIMS
83 Wacker Drive
Chicago, Illinois 60612

May 2

Leo Rosten
Apt. 39-A
Vesuvius Towers
644 E. 68 St.
New York, N.Y. 10021

Dear Leo:

Flo and me sure did applaud your answers to
our little girl who wrote up your Autobiography for
her Term Paper. "Pidge" said you must of been
kidding about some answers (like being born in
Coxsackie) but Flo said "If that is what he wrote
you, dear, that is what you should write! Writers
are famed for their eccentrics. And if Miss Ickelheimer raises any objections, just show her Leo's
letters—as prime-face evidence! Will you deny he is
the Last Word on his own lifes tale!!"

Youll never believe this, Leo, but Miss
Ickelheimer told "Pidge" after persuing her
Term Paper,--"That is the most interesting life-
story I have read in my 7-½ years as a teacher. I now
intend to read 1 or another of the books that man has
been author of!"

How about that, Leo! You have made a new
fan!!

Which brings me to the point of this epistle. I have told you how Pidge (Mildred) is a real nut about pidgeons. What I did not confide at that time is that Baby (Hortense) <u>hates</u> them. Baby even demanded that we either kill all of Pidges pidgeons or give her (Baby) a Parrott for Christmas! Which we did.

Leo, it is something to touch a heart of stone the way that kid loves that bird. She has taught the Parrott to say things like "Hello, sucker" and "Polly wants a cookie" (not "a cracker" the way other parrott-owners show no imagination in doing.)

We had one <u>bad</u> spell a few months back—when Pidge was teaching Babys parrott <u>on the sly</u> to say some pretty "fresh" words. Flo and me had to lay the Law down (to Pidge.) So now any of our friends will tell you they never heard a bird with such a refined vocabulery as Babys.

Which gets me to the point of this missive. Can you reccommend some good books about Parrotts for her to study? The School Librarian says that Baby has read the whole school stock in regard to Parrotts, of which they never had too many to begin with. So, do you know of any good ones? They have to be <u>reliable,</u> Leo, on account Baby knows so much about them she will spot a phoney item of information in a flash!!

Awaiting your prompt reply to this,

Your old school-mate,

"Herm"

P.S. If you have any books about Parrotts hanging around without you needing them anymore, maybe you can send them to Baby. Only send them to "Miss Hortense Klitcher". Just between the 2 of us, Baby hates it when someone (except I and Flo) calls her by that name.

"Herm"

LEO ROSTEN
Ornithology and Abscesses
706 Caligula Pit
New York, N.Y.

April 13

Herman P. Klitcher
Cinderella Laminated Shims
83 Wacker Drive
Chicago, Illinois 60612

Dear Herm:

Before I recommend any books on parrots, I
should know exactly what kind of parrot your Baby
owns. There are as many types of parrot as there are
types of type. The aviary order of Psittaciformes
happens to contain over 600 species and 100 genera,
generally specing. Some Psittaciformes live in the
tropics; others do not. But they all eat fruit, to
stay healthy.

The most important thing to remember, Herm,
is that parrots are oviparous vertebrates. This
does not mean that they hatch porous eggs in their
spines. It means they evaporate when placed in
vertical brates.

The Psittacidae, as insiders call the
larger grouping of these colorful creatures, consist not only of Parrots but include Cockatoos,
Macaws, Ka Kas, Kahapos, Lorikeets, and plain
Freaks. But all of them use their claws and beaks
when climbing—which is what distinguishes them
from every other order of bird in existence! One

<u>Psittacida</u> recently climbed Pike's Beak in 14 hours, without help from any motor vehicle.

You should warn Baby that parrots are not popular with other members of the feathered family called Aves, because they try harder. No one likes a show-off.

Finally, I hate to tell you this, Herm, but few people seem to realize that male parrots are "in heat" all the time! They do not have a mating "season." They are ready at any hour of day or night.

I would break this fact gently to Baby, if I were you; she is at an impressionable age, and you would not want her to sprout feathers.

Your old friend,

Leo

P.S. Can Hortense's pet whistle "Dixie"? Friends tell me that's a <u>dandy</u> tune for a parrot.

**From the Desk of
Herman P. Klitcher**

Apr. 18

Dear Leo:

Frankly, me and Flo could not tell if your
tech. dope about Parrots was on the level or just
spit-balling. (We saw thru the obvious funny stuff
like a shot!) So we asked Baby, who beleive you me,
buddy, knows her stuff where Aves are conserned!
And Baby said at least ¾ of your comments were
actually true and scientific. So we told her to
write you herself and thank you for all your ideas.
Boy, you sure do know the d--- things! Flo
went so far as to exclaim "Is there nothing that
man does not know some interesting aspic of, even
when in jest??"
I told her that was the kind of product
Crane Tech turned out in the old days!

Your buddy,

"*Herm*"

P.S. I enclose Babys note to you.

HORTENSE F. KLITCHER

Dear Mr. Rostan:

    Your stuff about Parrotts was marvy! Even
the put-ons. You do not have to re-answer.
    So—here goes a new question. I am fasinated
by the Toucan. What a collorful bird! But that
<u>enormous</u> beak! Why doesn't it toppel the Toucan
over?

                Wondering,

                Hortense

April 27

Dear Hortense:

Toucans certainly are colorful. They cause
heads to turn wherever they appear. As for their
beaks: The reason the toucan's beak does not topple
him over is that it is built (if you were to slice
it in half and look at the cross-section) like a
sponge, or a honey-comb. The beak is loaded with air.
It is therefore extremely light in weight. So much
for facts.

My private opinion is that the male toucan's beak plays a big role in courting the female.
That is what gave birth to the saying that toucan
live as cheaply as one.

Dreaming,

Mrs. Rostan

P.S. Did you ever think of making a pet out of a
numbat or a quokka? These delightful animals are
found in Australia. So is the bandicoot. Perhaps
your sister Mildred would consider switching from
pigeons to one of these.

From the Desk of
Herman P. Klitcher

Dear Leo—

Hey, pal! Hold it, for cryin-out-loud! I mean-stop futzing around with ideas in re the Pet dept.!

Migod, Leo, that kid ("Pidge") actually is going to the zoo and ask them about dumbats, bandecoots or animals like you told her sister about, but we never even heard of them!

Have a heart, Mac! Who wants a platoon of Quokkas quokking around their home?!?!

"Herm"

P.S. Flash! I am glad to say the Zoo did not have 1 sample of the animals you mentioned! They said such type rare creatures are best observed in their native habits. But now Mildred wants to go to Austrialia!!!

See what I mean, Leo?? Please get off your Yo-Yo. The Klitcher kids are patsys for your peculier type humor!

The 100%
Fool-Proof
Diet

June 2

Mr. Leo Rosten
Apt. 39-A
Vesuvius Towers
644 E. 68 St.
New York, N.Y. 10021

Cher Ami Leo:

When je pense of all the letters this year
that the various members of the Klitcher household
have sent to you, and the patient ways you have
responded to them even when in jest (and some of
your ideas are a scream!!) I feel my Hubby is a lucky
man to count someone of your type among his circle
of true friends! And the same goes for me. Even tho
we have not as yet met (which I feel safe in saying
each of us looks forward to that day) I feel as tho
I have known you most of my life! Do you get that
same feeling about me?

Well, I want to confide something, about a
personal matter and not a family problem. Leo, one
of the sad problems all of us (wherever we may reside)
face these days is—avoirdupois. I mean, getting
fat, which is a common problem amongst our age and
social set—especially the females, being in the

kitchen so much, cooking or to supervise the cook
(as it happens, Herm gives every luxury a husband
can provide his Loved Ones) with the result that
we nibble, nibble, <u>nibble</u> all day long. And this
puts pounds on us girls before we even turn around!

I don't have to tell you that taking off
weighth is agony! I know the smartest thing is not
to <u>put on</u> those pounds (you have to take off). But
that takes real will powers, which few of us can
boast of having enough of.

So I wonder if you, being in the World Center
of modern ideas, can advise us girls (well, <u>Me</u> in
partic!). What is the best way to bring your weighth
down on the scales? I mean without one of those
Diets it is real <u>torture</u> for a person to even try and
follow?! <u>Oui?</u>

Awaiting your reply, with sincere appre-
ciation in advance, I remain,

<u>Votre cher ami,</u>

Florence ("Flo") Klitcher

P.S. I have always wanted to ask you—does the
"Vesuvius" in your address pertain in any way to
the volcano—which is in or near Naples, Italy?

<u>Dietician Par Excellence</u>
7 Avoirdupois Allée
Beanpole
Nevada

June 16

Mrs. Herman P. Klitcher
210 Placebo Park
Euphoria, Illinois

<u>Cher</u> "Flo":

    I was beginning to wonder when I would hear
from you again. <u>Bon jour.</u>
    The answer to your question is quite simple:
The easiest way to bring your weight down on the
scales is to adjust the pointer. To lose five
pounds, for example, set the dial back five numbers;
to lose ten pounds, set it back ten numbers, and
so on.
    People to whom I have recommended this
simple, healthy method of weight-reduction have
gone to their graves smiling.
    I know what you mean about the ease with
which we add pounds as we get older. That is because
there is a destiny that ends our shapes. <u>C'est</u>
<u>triste,</u> I suppose, but that's <u>la vie.</u>
    But not all diets are "torture." The one
I use was described on a TV discussion, by a baseball
or football player (it is sometimes hard to tell
the games apart in the Manhattan area): At each

meal, put into your mouth any type and quantity of
food you love. If you follow one rule in this diet,
Flo, you will never gain an ounce! The rule is simple: Don't swallow.

A bientôt,

Leo Rosten

P.S. "Vesuvius Towers" is just the name of the hi-
rise in which I reside. (People do not "live" in
New York anymore: they survive there.)
     The reason my apartment house carries such
a colorful name is that the builder, who was Italian,
was homesick. He pined for mother love, which he
pronounced in English as "lava." Heaven knows
there's plenty of that around Vesuvius.

June 20

Leo Rosten
39-A Vesuvius Towers
644 East 68 Street
New York, N.Y. 10021

Dear Leo—

Your letter about Diets had us all in
stitches!! I read your memento aloud to our Cannasta
Club, and the way those girls laughed we were rolling
in the isles!

The ministers daughter named "Jehoada"
(after some character in the Bible no one ever <u>heard</u>
of, which is why we call her "Jerry") went his-
terical over your Diet advice, about putting anything in your mouth you want, in any amounts thereof,
only—"Do not swallow!" <u>Laugh?!</u> No one has heard
"Jerry" laugh like that since her husband died.
(Last June.)

Leo, if you had not turned into an Author you
could have made a real Comedian! On a par with people
like Rudy Shmelzer or "Buckets" Blood, who are
tops as entertainers in "Fanny's Hide-a-way," the

night club our gang frequently frequents on a dull
Saturday night in Euphoria.

Anyway, to stop rambeling around ten bushes
(which Hermie says I do)—Can you help our Penelope,
who is taking an exam at Shimmel High where she is a
Junior, next week? She is so mixed-up on one part
that I begged her to ask you for the answer to a question she is sure Mr. Diefenfuss (the teacher giving
that exam) will spring on the class.

Penelope is a real doll, Leo, called "Bubbles" (as I have told you) by her chums ever since
she was in dipers. (The reason we named her "Penelope" in the first place was because we just loved
the nickname of "Penny"—but no one caught on to
that, and began calling her "Bubbles", which she
hates but has stuck to her. It just goes to show, you
can never predict how a public will act, n'est ce
pas?)

So "Penny" is just too shy to write a
famous person like you. So I coxed her to write out
the problem she is scared of (in the forth-coming
exam) and I would pass it on to you!! That is why you
will find her problem inclosed in this envelope.

Please answer fast, as that exam is breathe-
ing down all our necks. Avec gratitude toujours,

Your friend,

"Flo"

P.S. Forgetting diets, can you give me some tips
about just Keeping Fit?

LEO ROSTEN
Physical Therapist
98.6 Thermometer Drive
Utopia
Texas

                                                    June 27

Mon Cher Flo:

        The best way to keep fit, in my experience,
is this: After lunch each day, take a brisk, long
nap.

                                    Yours,

                                    Leo

P.S. I will answer "Penny" as soon as I digest the
fascinating letter you enclosed.

Polyunsaturated
Fats
Exposed!

To Mr. Leo Roston Esq.
(by via my mother, Mrs. Florence P. Klitcher)

      Mr. Roston, can you help me on what is the basic way to learn the difference between Saturated and Polly-<u>un</u>saturated Fats? I am in summer school, making up a certain flunk.

      I have read the chapter in our text-book which explains that problem 'til I am blue in the face —but I just can't get it into my head! I am really confused by the <u>complex</u> stuff about Carbon Molecules and Fatty Acids and the "double-chain with Hydro-gen" so that they become unsaturated, and so forth.

      I am sure that with your gifts of explain-ing, Mr. Roston, you can make this as clear as a bell, or better, to even I.

      Please make the explanation <u>simple</u>, not technicel, as I am a long way from being Mr. Diefen-fuss, our teacher, or even Mr. Lempke, our druggist, who I have tried to discuss this with but with no luck.

      I am very grateful for any enlightining you can shed on this subject. And so will my friends, probly.

Your admirer,

Penelope ("Penny") Klitcher

LEO ROSTEN
Professor of Chemistry
Bunsen Burner Drive
Pharmacologia
South Dakota

July 4

Miss Penelope Klitcher
210 Placebo Park
Euphoria, Illinois

Dear Penny:

You ask "What is the basic way to learn the difference between saturated and polyunsaturated fats?" The best way is to do your homework. That will give you the unsaturated facts.

My way of distinguishing saturated from unsaturated fats can be put in a nutshell. For best results, the nutshell should be about the size of a walnut.

Pour the fat you are unsure about into this nutshell: If the fat is saturated, the shell will turn pink. If the fat is unsaturated, the shell will break out in goose-pimples. And if the fat is Poly-unsaturated, the shell will bulge in the middle, looking roly-poly, which is why it received such a curious name.

Notice that words like "saturated," "unsaturated," "statutory," or "Staten Island" all contain more than one "t". They are all acids, which tea is, too. Any dictionary will tell you that the technical name for tea, <u>Thea sinensis</u>, is derived from Chinese, Latin and Thai. That is why people who become addicted to the taste of tea-bags, and cannot get them except from criminal pushers, break into such a sweat that we say they are "fit to be Thaid."

If you want more technical answers, Penny, ones you can use for Mr. Diefenfuss's exam (<u>and</u> discuss with Mr. Lempke), I am happy to offer them. You must be patient, though, because the answers, although very simple, are very complicated.

1) Fatty acids consist of four elements:

Carbon

Hydrogen

Carboxyl

Licorice

These acids are arranged in a chain, which is visible under any microscope. The carbon molecules form the chain; the hydrogen molecules dangle from it, like souvenirs.

Now comes the crucial part, Penny:

2) If the carbon molecules are attached to each other, and show it by smiling or terms of endearment, they are called "saturated." <u>But</u>—

3) When a chain of carbon molecules is double-chained, it has no room for any hydrogen, and is called "unsaturated." Mind you, unsaturated fats are not <u>sad,</u> they are just not saturated with friendly feelings to or from other molecules.

4) Where the carbon elements try to make a mountain out of a molecule, they will reject the friendly overtures of hydrogen particles and are called "polyunsaturated." This means that the carbons have become so spoiled by flattering propositions that they have turned frigid and won't

let themselves be saturated by anyone. Carbons are not very original.

If you depict all of this on a chart, you are sure to make a big impression on Mr. Diefenfuss (and possibly give Mr. Lempke a nervous breakdown):

Carbon and Hydrogen Components in

<u>MOLECULAR CHARTS</u>

of

<u>THE FATTY ACID FAMILY</u>

CHART 1. SATURATED FATS

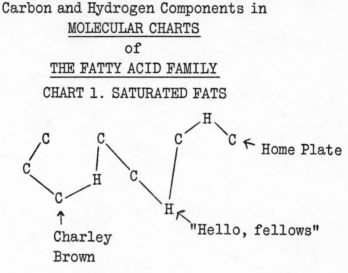

CHART 2. UNSATURATED COUSINS

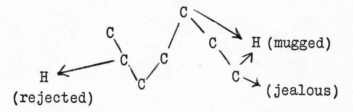

3. POLYUNSATURATED (Relatives from Out of Town)

That is a map of Australia.

I trust this answers all your questions.
Good luck with the exam.

Your friendly bio-chemist

Leo Rootsm

P.S. What ever happened to "Slats"? And "Chico"!

The
Handy-Dandy
Human Brain

Cinderella LAMINATED SHIMS
83 Wacker Drive
Chicago, Illinois 60612

Aug. 8

Leo Rosten
Apt. 39-A
Vesuvius Towers
644 East 68 St.
New York, N.Y.

Dear Leo:

Sometimes after we persue one of your epistles, me and Flo sit up for hours wondering—
"Is Leo "putting us on"?"
"Is he kidding 100%—or only in some
places?"
"Is he nuts?"
"Or just acting cute the way humorists are
suppose to?"
This is not easy to answer, pal, because
just when we are sure you are throwing us a line of
bull (like with that technicel stuff about Poly-
unsatturates, Carbon of Dioxide, or the Hummbold
Current) we ask Alvin or Penelope to look it up in a
reliable Reference book—and find out you were
giving us some real MacCoy!!! (In parts.) We appreciate that right down to the hilt. It is only the
stuff that is jokery or just futzing around that
bugs us.

238

Anyways, something came up at our Bridge Turnament the other night, when we were at the Howie Hasseltrouts (it being their turn to supply the feed.) In between 1 thing and the other, Luther Ponash pops this question, which I know will grab you. (Luther and Holly Ponash have a son Gilbert at Purdue U. who took a powder. They were nawing their finger-nails til they found he had joined the Peace Crops and was in some far-away jungle Doing Good for the Natives (which was O.K., him not being a full-time bum like some Euphorians sons). Then that crud Gil gets a Thing for a very short native girl, and he writes home how will his folks feel if he marries her and brings her home? Well, Holly Ponash colapsed, so Luther tried to put the kibosh on—cabeling Gil that a Thing is 1 thing but to Marry is another when the bride happens to come from a tribe where if he (Gil) ever wants to leave her she will eat him . . . They havnt heard a peep from Gil.)

So lets return to Luthers real grabber at the Hasseltrouts—

"Can anyone here explain in a Laymans words how Electronic Computers actualy work?"

Leo, I have to admit I could not answer— even allthough I took Geometry at Crane Tech, where you will remember that was no snap.

I may be going off half-crocked to ask you a thing like this, pal, computers not being up an authors alley. So you can just bow out with a brief note of apology if you are ignorant of the answer. And me and Flo will not hold it against you.

But I have a hunch that you out of all the guys I know can answer Luthers question in a way a Layman or Laywoman (thats no pun, ha, ha, but it sure could be, if you know some of the female types that infest any Suburb, even in Euphoria) will get thru

their skull!! A <u>simple</u> explanation of—How does
a Computer really work? And what makes them call it
"Dijital"?

I sure would like to make Luther Ponashs 2 eyes
pop out of his head!

Thanks loads, buddy
Herman ("Herm") P. Klitcher

P.S. Maybe you could draw a simple chart to explain
the principal.

"Herm"

LEO ROSTEN
President
Cybernetics and Halvah, Inc.
1400 Solid State Drive
Short Circuit
New Jersey

Sept. 24

Herman P. Klitcher
Cinderella Laminated Shims, Inc.
83 Wacker Drive
Chicago, Ill. 60612

Dear Herm:

I have just returned from a month in Erie, so
I certainly can explain how a digital computer
works. And you were quite shrewd to suggest I do it
by chart. If anything can make Luther Ponash's eyes
pop (though I can't guarantee they both will pop out
as far as you desire, considering all he has gone
through) it is a chart.

But first, Herm, you ask why these wonderful
computers are called "digital." The reason is that
they make it possible for people to count without
using their fingers. As you know, people have been
counting on their digits for centuries. Some book-
keepers actually counted their fingers to the bone,
and children who bit their nails found it hard to do
fractions. That is why educators ever since Maria
Montessori had been urging mathematicians to de-

velop an automatic device that would banish finger-counting forever.

The first automatic computer was invented by Antoine Czermak, a Czech who worked in a bank. Czermak got so fatigued from distinguishing "checks" from "Czechs" hour after hour six days a week, that he built a special cross-checking machine.

It worked like a charm—except where foreign exchange was involved: The gadget kept translating English pounds into 32 ounces, and sent francs to a meat-packer in Hamburg. When this was discovered by a big cheese in the Swiss bank, poor Czermak killed himself in mortification, a small town near the Austrian border.

The next important step in automatic computation was a machine devised by Piotr Kropotkin, the famous Esthonian bugler, whose fingers had given out after 26 years of playing the Esthonian national anthem. Kropotkin's counting machine cleverly used compressed air, instead of batteries. Where it failed was in handling decimal points, since it is an old Esthonian custom never to point at a decimal. Kropotkin ended up in a mental institution.

The great computer breakthrough came in our own country (and we can all be mighty proud of that, Herm) in 1946, when Shlomo Omo, a mathematical wizard in one of our Think-tanks, discovered that by using simple "On-Off" wall switches, he could create an entirely new numerical vocabulary, consisting of out-witted mathematic symbols. Omo's trick lay in treating "On" as "1," and "Off" as "0." By arranging and extending these two digits, any number could be translated into the new computer language! For example:

```
00 = 0
01 = 1
11 = 2
10 = 3
101 = 4
111 = 5
```

and so on. A number like 7,436 (the average tonnage
of cod-trawlers in Iceland) involved a great many
figures (10111001010100001001111111010100001, to be
exact)—but Omo's computer worked at electronic
speed. As a result, Omo, trying to keep up with it,
had a heart-attack. His work was carried on by his
wife, Selma, and in no time at all her application of
Shlomo's dazzling digitry brought the marvelous
new world of electronic computers into being. They
have been there ever since.

Now to the chart: The first thing to bear in
mind, Herm, is that a computer works exactly the
way your brain does—and just as simply. If you will
study the diagram (below) everything should be
crystal clear.

An Idea enters the brain (or computer)
shortly before lunch, and is quickly sped to Central
Control (A) where it is scanned and classified to
distinguish it from hiccoughs. Central Control
relays the Idea to Lost-and-Found (B), which
promptly signals an impulse-messenger (Fred) who

goes to point R, where he gets off and waits for the #78 bus. This bus takes him to P.S. 41, where he is sure to find a Principal.

Note: In order for the brain or computer to work with the speed and efficiency explained above, it is important to check all relays for cavities. A computer with a neglected cavity will act pretty strange, Herm. The one they used at R.K.O., before it went bankrupt, cracked pistachio nuts.

I hope this clears everything up.

Your old buddy,

Leo

**From the Desk of
Herman P. Klitcher**

Sept. 22

Dear Leo:

    That chart of yours is just plain <u>nutsy,</u>
if you ask me!
    Were you trying to be comical? Flo and me
gave up after failing to figure out why the Impulse-
Messenger has to be named "Fred."
    Leo, <u>were you goofing off again</u> or <u>what??</u>
Je-<u>zus</u>!

       Your pal

       "Herm"

From the
Desk
of
Leo Rosten

Sept. 30

Dear Desk of H.P.K.:

     Impulse-messengers are known as "Fred"
throughout the computer world because the man
who invented them was a young Hawaiian named
Frances Edelforth. If you join "F" and "r" to
"ed" you come up with the acronym "Fred."
(Scientists adore acronyms, and keep a master
list in Akron, Ohio.)
     I think you and Flo will be interested in
knowing that the mathematicians at Cal Tech wanted
to call the Impulse-Messengers "Derf," which is
"Fred" spelled backwards, but they changed their
minds when a detergent of that name exploded in the
M.I.T. lab. That fouled up the computers so badly
that it took 216 Maoists, working their abacuses
for 18 months, to locate the error.

     —Desk of L.R.

**From the Desk of
Herman P. Klitcher**

Dear Leo—

    I know when Im being had!!

                     "*Herm*"

P.S. Flo could not find 1 single detergent named
"Derf"—and that was in the best super-market
in Euphoria.

From the
Desk
of
Leo Rosten

Dear Desk:

    So do I.

P.S. In any supermarket worthy of the name, "Derf"
is kept next to "Lash."

Mrs. Herman P. Klitcher
201 Placebo Park
Euphoria, Ill. 60035

Leo Rosten
Apt. 39-A
Vesuvius Towers
644 E. 68 St.
New York, N.Y. 10021

<u>Cher, cher ami!</u>

      The way you and Hermie carry on—! Honestly!
You are grown men, not <u>garcons</u>.
      Who makes "Lash"? I would like to try it.
The name is perfect for a detergent.

                    <u>Toujours,</u>

                    "*Fl.*"

LEO ROSTEN
R.F.D. 2
Repel Dirt Road
Alabaster
Alabama

Mrs. Herman P. Klitcher
210 Placebo Park
Euphoria, Illinois

Très cher Flo:

        "Lash" is made by a company in Chicago
called (I believe) Cinderella. "Lash" is an
acronym for "laminated shims."

                                Toodle-oo,

                                Leo

The
Sad Case of
Gloria Bleacher

Cinderella LAMINATED SHIMS
83 Wacker Drive
Chicago, Illinois 60612

Nov. 8

Leo Rosten
Apt. 39-A
Vesuvius Towers
644 E 68 St.
New York, N.Y. 10021

Dear Leo—

You have to be kidding! I was all rawed up
(after your latest memento on the Human Brain) so
I started to dictate a pretty nasty straight-from-
the-sholder reply. But you are lucky, on account my
new Sec. is takeing her 1½ hour Coffee Brake—so I
cooled down and will not even ignore your screw-ball
type humor!

Your buddy in spite of it,

"Herm"

P.S. I had to give the heave-ho to my Sec.—Miss
Gloria Bleacher, when I found out she was afraid of
carbon paper. The amount of them she destroyed (before even useing them) would make you cry! If there
was 1 little wrinkel or caress on a sheet of bran-new
carbon, Gloria Bleacher crumpeled it up in her fist
at once, praticaly strangling it with glee!

Leo, by 11 A.M. each day her waist-basket
was so piled up with crumpled black balls it looked
like a tar pit. Plus, that made her have to go to the
Ladies 2-3 times an hour—to wash the smudjes off
her Lily White hands and fingers.

I warned her 30-40 times that if Mr. Krumbach (who watches every penny of expenses or employ-
ees goofing off) got wise, it was Good-by, Gloria
Bleacher. And that is what happened.

What a lousy break for me.

Just between the 2 of us (and I know you
would never blab a peep about this to Flo) I hated to
see her (Gloria) go. She was a good typist—besides
having a pair of nockers you could admire from any
angel. And legs—man, I better not go into her legs!
They were like Marlene Dietricks gams in the oldie
"The Blue Angle". How often in a man's career does
he get a Sec. like that?? She even spelled most words
right.

If only she wasnt afraid of carbon paper.

et

LEO ROSTEN
Personnel Consultant
(Secretaries - Filing Clerks - Receptionists)
707 Pittman Way
Hallelujah
Tennessee

PRIVATE AND CONFIDENTIAL

Nov. 12

Herman P. Klitcher
Cinderella Laminated Shims
83 Wacker Drive
Chicago, Ill. 60612

Dear Herm—

Would Miss Bleacher consider a job in New York?

Yours,

Leo

Should a Girl
Use Bad,
Bad Words?

Cinderella LAMINATED SHIMS
83 Wacker Drive
Chicago, Illinois 60612

Nov. 18

Leo Rosten
Apt. 39-A
Vesuvius Towers
644 E. 68 St.
New York, N.Y.10021

Dear Leo:

The way you answer questions can make a guy
hystericel! (I do not mean funny hystericel but from
frusteration!) You go all the way around Robins Hood
Barn instead of giving a direct type answer. That
is not helpfull!! At all. And those crazy addresses
you go right on cooking up. They are the End!
So try and lay off the jokery this time. It
is about something that has me and Flo in a real bind.
About Hortense (who we call "Baby") and who is going on 13.
She is a nice kid, Leo, and pretty when her
mouth is shut so you dont see all the wire-braces and
rubber-bans that are setting me back a <u>fortune</u> for
the fancy Orothodenotist Flo found (and I cant say
Im crazy about him.) One or two crooky teeth never
hurt a girl in my time or yours, so whats all this
modern dental agony?
But get back to "Baby." She was doing

<u>great</u> in school, but now her teacher sends us a note
regarding Hortenses being a "problem"! And what
type "problem" did Miss Ickelheimer (her teacher)
have in mind, to send such an up-setting missive to
her mother and I? What crime has Hortense accom-
plished? Does she fart in class like "Sooky"
Popov? Or throw sour-balls at 1 and all like
"Fatso" Dobish (a holy terrier)?? Or things of
that ilk? O no! Miss Ickelheimer says our Hortense
has been useing 1 or 2 "bad" words in class (when
fighting with some other kid.)

 Well, that only puts our Baby in the same
boat as all the other brats you see these days, is my
personal opinion. But still it is real up-setting to
Flo, who you have not had the pleasure of meeting,
who is a very neat type about speech, sex, and etc.
As for your old buddy "Herm"—around my own tribe
I watch my lingo like God is right there in the room,
in person, spying on me 24 hours per day!!!

 So where does our Baby hear the bad words
Miss Ickelheimer is crabbing about? (She would not
even give us a sample, so we could know what to look
out for.) She must be hearing that fowl language from
the other kids!! Right? So in <u>that</u> case the blame is
on Shimmel Hi and the type <u>parents</u> who let their kids
use words of the type you hear in the movies these
kids are allowed to go and see!! Leo, some of these
flicks are full of such <u>disgusting</u> words Flo and me
can hardly wait for "THE END" to appear on the
screen sos we can walk out in indigination.

 So why blame Baby? Fair is fair. Right?
Still, me and Flo now keep a sharp ear out.

 Take the other night. Right after the family
meal. I ask "Baby, please take out the garbadge."

 She replies "O ----. I am busy."

 I am shocked stiff (allthough ---- is not

the worst type word she could of used). But I hide
my dismay to say "Taking out garbadge is your job,
Baby, your "chore" as it is called. Every kid takes
garbadge out to help their own parents!"

Hortense looks at me like I am a monster
from outward space and says "Why dont you get off my
back?" And before I can drive the lesson home she
is on the "hot line" with Sooky Popov, yakking it up
about some Hi-Fi records they play so loud you think
they are broadcasting to Moscow.

Or take the time last week, during the
"Cocktail Hour" when Flo and me have our Martinis.
Hortense was in her own room, as usual playing Rock
music that makes me wonder if the Nazis are bombard-
ing London again.

I say "Flo, can Miss Ickelheimer be right?
Have you noticed how our little girl is begining
to use certain bad words lately?"

"It is not lately, Lover" replys Flo
moodily "and she is not begining. She passed her
Learners Permit and is ready to graduate with
Honors."

"Then why have you not done anything about
it?!!" I cry.

"Like what?" snaps Flo.

"Like telling her to stop!!"

"I have told her to stop 50 times if its a
day!" cracks Flo.

"Then whenever she uses a bad word slap her
across the kisser!" I imply.

"And rune $800 worth of dental re-construc-
tion?!" asks Flo.

"O G-- do not swat her that hard" I protest
"Just enough to make her stop!"

"Your darling happens to be exceptionaly
quick in ducking" Flo says.

So I head for the Martini pitcher.

"I will tell you something worse" Flo
glooms as she follows my suit "Our Baby is now using
certain words to the very face of our guests!!" and
Flo pores herself a replacement like she is fullback
for the Chicago Bears. "Did you hear what sne said
to Mrs Frobisher?"

"Who is Mrs Frobisher?" I inquire.

"That fancy Society Lady who came here,
into our home, to tell me about their Church Raffel."

"I was not here" I observe.

"Thats why you did not hear what transpired" says Flo.

"When was it?" I ask.

"Last Friday" informs Flo.

"Last Friday I was in Peoria, to put the
heat on "Toby" Samoosh, who fell far below his sales
quota."

"You should of been home and do your duty
as a father!" accuses Flo.

"I would not have a home if I did not put my
work ahead of it" I retort.

"Do not rub it in" says Flo.

"Tough titty" I offer.

"It was terrible! I blush to even think of
what Hortense said to Mrs. Frobisher" said Flo
turning the color of ketchup.

"Blush all you want" I snort "But tell me—
what did Hortense actualy say?!"

Well, Leo, Flo puts down what was resently
a Martini and she covers both cheeks with her hands—
which makes her look like shes on fire, on account
of the Flaming Passion nail-polish she uses (on
her nails.) And in a choked-up or boozy voice Flo
says "Mrs. Cynthia Frobisher was in this very room
and asked your Baby "And what is your ambition,

little girl?" And your Little Angel answers "To
"make out" with every boy in the class.!!"

"My God!" I pray, heading for the bottle.

Flo beats me to the pain-killer and says
"If my Father ever hears about that comment by
Baby, Lover-Boy, you will get thrown out of your
job at Cinderella right on your can!"

"He will not hear of it from me!" I promise.

"He is coming over Sunday!" Flo reminds me
"Alone."

"Then lets send Baby over to your sister!"
I advise.

"Like h---!" Flo hiccupps. "Daddy will
crack his hernia if his pet Grandchild is not here to
fling her little arms around him and laugh at all
his jokes!"

"Then we must beg Baby to be on her best
behavior!" I exclaim.

"You beg her" Flo snorts "I am getting
Hot Flushes from her."

"She is your kid as well as mine!" I shout
"A mother is suppose to raise the kids—"

"That brat can't be raised; she has to be
fumigated!" Flo declares.

"That is a funny remark, I have to admit" I
admit as I refill our glasses.

"You have imbibed too much booze" says Flo.

"You are pretty stinko yourself" I reply.

And at this very point, Leo, what do we hear
but the voice of none other than our Baby! She has
been right there standing in the doorway. Grinning
"Are you 2 loaded again?"

"Do not use a vulgar word like "loaded" in
my presents!" snaps Flo.

"Language your watch in front of your
mother" I manage, like a jerk.

"Ch-ripes" grins Baby "Even your sentenses comes out a-- backwards."

"Go to your room and stay there!" Flo bombs her "Until you learn to behave with good manners!"

Which is what I have been begging Hortense to do (through her key-hole) all day—without her making a word of reply. Her Hi-Fi is turned on to 1 number, over and over, that is called "Sock It To Me, Hot Hips" and was not composed by Guy Lombardo.)

So thats why I am taking up my pen again, Leo. What should we do? (About Baby?)

Me and Flo pride ourselfs on being progres- sive-type parents, and realize that a child has certain unalien civil rights, just the same as you. So I don't want to hit her or use my brute strenth. But begging and begging her to "clean up" her speech has not helped. And we realise we have to cure Baby of the phaze she is going thru before it is to late!

Leo, what do those Child Psychologists you know advise a parent to do in such a case??

Awaiting your anxious reply.

Your old pal,

Herman ("Herm") Fletcher

P.S. Please answer fast and with no flack, as we are on pins and needels.

"H"

LEO ROSTEN
Sump Pumps And Child Guidance
392 Wisteria Lane
Groin Falls
West Virginia

Nov. 22

Mr. Herman Klitcher
Vice-President
Cinderella Laminated Shims, Inc.
83 Wacker Drive
Chicago, Ill. 60612

Dear Herm:

I know little about child psychologists,
never having consulted one under 48; but I think
parents should never beg a 12-year-old to do anything. Tell her. (Then let her have it.)

I realize that, being progressive parents,
you and Flo feel that Hortense has a right to use
the same language you do. That is true. But if actual profanity is involved, she only has the right
to swear at herself. (She can do this in her room,
in the shower, or—if she has theatrical ambitions—
in front of a mirror.)

If "Baby" wants to swear at you or her
mother Flo (what are the names of her other mothers?)
tell her (Hortense) that she will have to pay for the
pleasure and privilege: say, a dollar a word. I
will be glad to come over and let her swear at me
at these rates. You and Flo will be surprised by how

sensible a child becomes the moment cash is involved.

One couple I know, the Olaf Huttschneckers,
followed my advice and made their 16-year-old daughter, Iolanthe, "pay by the word." Within a month
Olaf put in a water softener from the allowance
money saved. In fact, the Huttschneckers chuckled
merrily whenever Iolanthe used an unclean word.
They even began to encourage Iolanthe to use bad
words, and within a fortnight they had salted away
enough fine-money to put an electric mosquito-
trap on their porch. By the end of the year, the
Huttschneckers had saved enough money to move to
a better neighborhood, leaving Iolanthe behind.

When Iolanthe reached 18, and found her
way back to her parents' home, the Huttschneckers
began to swear at her. I have never seen a family
with closer mutual understanding.

Your old friend,

Leo

Have a good Thanksgiving.

Nov. 29

Dear Leo:

At first me and Flo were pretty d--- sore about your missive (in regard to our bad-words problem with Hortense). But you know what? We finaly tried your advise, and told "Baby" it would cost her a buck ($1.00) each time she let a vulgar expression escape her lips. It took no more than 6 bucks worth that Hortense saw we meant Business! She is watching her speech now like she is getting ready to join a Convent!!!

So me and Flo have solved the problem with no help from anybody, thanks to you! This time without clowning, you really came thru!! You have showed what true pal-ship can be!!

Your buddy,

"*Herm*"

P.S. In answer to your peculier question—Baby has only the 1 mother! <u>Flo</u> is her mother. I cant figure out what makes you ask that type <u>crazy</u> question.
P.P.S. I am her father.

Why Do
Parents
Nag, Nag, Nag?

HORTENSE KLITCHER

Dec. 23

Dear Mr. R.—

        Why do my Parents nag, nag, nag, <u>nag</u> me all
the time???

                        Your friend

                        Hortense ("Baby")

Merry Xmas, I hope.

Dec. 30

Dear "Baby":

    I don't know, know, know, <u>know.</u>

             Your friend,

              Jive

Happy New Year, I know.

Never Name
a Dog
Aaron

ALVIN J. KLITCHER
210 Placebo Park
Euphoria
Ill.

Jan. 16

Leo Rosten
Apt. 39-A
Vesuvius Towers
644 E. 68 St.
New York, N.Y. 10021

Dear Mr. Rosten:

I wouldn't have the nerve to right to you
again—except my Father and Mother (Mr. and Mrs.
Herman P. Klitcher) tell me you are a great guy in
regard to re-helping old friends, and tho I am only 17
so can't be one I want to ask you about a thing that is
real close to my heart—that being my Dog.

As you maybe have heard from my Dad or Mom,
we Klitchers are a real Pet-lover family, with
everyone having one all of his own. Like my one
sister with a Parrot and the other raising pidgeons
(Yech!) and "Bubbles" with boys, who she acts like
they are not human but pets. And me, with my pooch.

I have had this dog since he was a pup—when
even then, tho he licked everybody on the hand, face,
hands or other places where there are no clothes,
he was still kind of stupid. He is now 8 years old and
no smarter! In fact I have to say that even as his

fellow Cocker Spaniells go (which he is) he is a
dumbell.

Here is just one example of many I could.
When any member of our family comes home he (or she)
will call out "Hey Aaron! Here boy! Come on Aaron.
Lets see that friendly puss. Here Aaron, Aaron,
Aaron, Aaron!!"

Well, Aaron does not come, Mr. Rosten—to
me or my Father or Hortense or to anyone. Even when
called by name! Instead of jumping up and licking
your cheeks, hands or face he just stays wherever
he happens to be at that moment, and he will not bark
or jump up or run around yapping like all other dogs
do. He just stays where he is. Mopeing is the best
way I know to describe it. Or if at the time he is
snoozing, he purrs and purrs, without his opening up
an eye. Yet he will not give his own master (me) the
time of day! I think this is a very undog-like way for
a dog to behave.

So here is my question. How can I make Aaron
more doglike in his conduct, and not just mope
around the house like every day is a national holiday
for animals! Not even opening one eye up and snoozing
in front of the fire even in July, when we don't even
have a fire going there! Is not Aaron's behavior
peculier?

I need your help on this! For which I thank
you.

Son of your old buddy,

Alvin ("Al") J. Kitcher

February 2

Dear Alvin:

In my opinion, your dog is not stupid but moody. I think he just does not like to be called Aaron.

Dogs are extremely sensitive creatures, Al, and calling one by a name he hates is likely to create deep emotional conflicts within his psyche.

Furthermore, when you or your father calls "Here, Aaron! Here, Aaron, Aaron, Aaron, Aaron!" this makes Aaron feel like a dope who doesn't know his own name and has to be reminded of it five times. I suggest you cut down on the number of Aarons.

The most interesting part of your description is that Aaron "purrs." Are you sure he is purring? I think he is burring. When an Aaron burrs, he is trying to tell you something—and I don't blame him. How would you like to be reminded, every time someone enters your house, that you have the same first name as the dastard who killed Alexander Hamilton? I don't think you can expect a dog to lick the hands or face of anyone who makes him feel like a traitor.

The best cure for Aaron is to send him to a good school where he can study American history. In that way, he will learn about other Aarons in our past—good, patriotic Aarons, Aarons with whom he can identify and thus find happiness. (I can't think of such an Aaron off-hand, but I am an authority on dogs, not history.)

Finally, Alvin, never ask a dog to show you his "puss." Nothing confuses an animal more than nomenclature which is alien to his species. If you ask a dog to "show his puss" all through his formative years, he is bound to wonder whether he is a dog or a cat. Naturally, he would not know whether to bark or meow. After eight years of such an identity crisis, Aaron is playing it safe. He knows that he has the features of a dog, but adjusts to his environment; whenever asked to show his puss, he purrs. Al, you have a pooch of remarkable adaptive powers there.

I would suggest you change Aaron's name. There are many well-established names for dogs— names which they love, and to which they have for centuries responded ecstatically (jumping up and down, licking the hands or cheeks of whoever pronounces the name properly, etc.). I am sure you know a dozen names fit for a dog, but if you need suggestions here are a few: Spot, Rex, Tiger, Sunshine, King. (I would not call a dog Queen or Queenie unless he is a she.)

The name should fit the dog's personality. An energetic dog should not be called Lazybones, for instance, since that would undermine his initiative. A sullen dog should not be called Smiles or Happy, which he would regard as sarcasm—and, as is well-known, sarcasm drives any dog to temper-tantrums.

In the case of Aaron, whose personality is pretty well established by this time, you might try such names as Coma, Prone, or Manger. Any of these seems to fit Aaron's temperament to a "t."

    I am confident that once you change Aaron's
name, and use it with patient, loving care, he will
surprise you by reversing his undoglike behavior.
I know of one case where a dog named Achilles kept
snapping at people's heels. When the family changed
Achilles' name to Spitz, he swam the English
Channel.

                              Yours,

                              Leo Rosten

P.S. Incidentally, it is wrong to expect Aaron to
give you the time of day. Dogs do not know how to tell
time. Very few animals do, except for those put into
Swiss clocks. Owls, who are supposed to be so damn
smart, can only tell when it is night-time—and
that's no big deal, if you ask me, since they are
blind as bats in the daytime.
    If you decide to call your dog "Broadway,"
give him my regards.

SHOOTING THE BREEZE WITH

"AL" KLITCHER

March 4

Dear Mr. Rosten—

      I have read your letter to my Dad and Mom
and after a long arguement decided to re-name my
dog "KLITCH"—which has worked out pretty good
(so far.) That is why I have not answered you before.
      We felt Aaron would not know we are calling
him if we used a real new name like "Manger" (our
#2 choice) as that would be to big a change from his
present. But as he has heard the name of "Klitcher"
so many times (while evesdropping on the phone, or
observing what the maleman calls us on delivering
packages etc.) we figured the name of "Klitch"
would at least have a familiar ring to him.
      So we are not calling Aaron Aaron anymore.
And we sure are gratefull to you for a real nifty
idea in regard to what has been bothering Aaron all
of these years.

Your new pal,

"Al" K.

P.S. Klitch has just begun to growel!! He does not
<u>bark</u> as yet, but I think a growel is better then a
purr. Don't you?

March 11

Dear "AL"—

No, I do not purr. But I agree that a growl,
in Aaron's case, is a step in the right direction.
Good work, Al!
Keep your eyes peeled for one thing: Dogs
called "Klitch" are likely to start grinding
their teeth, and your Dad has pretty strong ideas
about orthodontists' bills.

Your pal,

— L. R.

Mar. 26

Dear Mr. R—

Don't worry about doggy-dentist bills.

That pooch has run away! 8 days now and no
Aaron. I think he is heading for Canada.

At first I was very sore at you, Mr R. for
making me change the name of Aaron to "Klitch"!
which I think made Aaron head for the border. But
my Father reminds me you only said to change Aaron's
name and did not say to make it "Klitch". So now I
blame my-self for giving a dog a name that drove him
away from his own home.

I was so broke-up about this that I called
Stella Ockels, who is the Big-Brain in our class.
But as luck would not have it, Stella was not home
but was taking her Flute lesson.

So I went for a moody walk to try and overcome my sorrows—and who do I run into but Barby
Revere, the most beateous chick at Shimmel Hi, by
actual vote. "Why are you looking so down-on your
mouth?" she inquires.

So I tell her, which I would never had the
nerve to do without her making the first move. So
she says, "Come into my house and let your hair
down." Wow!

Inside of 2 minutes flat in her nearby home
I saw that Barby really dug me—in a way no one of her
sex before ever has. Did she turn me on!! Crazy!

        And I began to feel grateful to Aaron for his
treachery! If not for him I would not be the Star in
Barby's eyes (and she has many). I guess it is true
that every clod has a silver lining.
        So it's all hanging out with Al Klitcher.
I don't even miss that dum pooch Aaron. I have a new
pet (you can say)—a beauteus "bird"! who any
jock will tell you you can have a <u>ball</u> with better
than a dog any day (or night, ha, ha!)

                                Your friend

                                "Al"

P.S. It's a real break Stella Ockels was not home but
licking her flute when I dingle-ingled her, for <u>she</u>
is a dog (as we say).

                        —*"Al"*

A Plague
of
Grasshoppers

Mrs. Herman P. Klitcher
201 Placebo Park
Euphoria, Ill. 60035

July 6

Mr. Leo Rosten
Apt. 39-A
Vesuvio Tours
644 E. 68 St.
New York, N.Y. 10021

"Cher ami" Leo:

     Je vous ecrivez because we have run into a
horrible problem in our beautiful Suburb—which
is a plage of grasshoppers like you never in your
whole life saw before!
     Mon ami, these Insects are so big they come
at you in hords! They make that story in the Bible
take a back seat, and even out-do the scene in Cecil
B. DeMill's movie about the 10 Commandments, which
I am sure you saw, where there is that terrible plage
of lotuses. Or even the great one where Humphrey
Bogart is swatting away at those horrible flying
creatures who are attacking him and K. Hepburn, to
give them real panic and shivers, The African's
Queen—one of Herm and mine favorite oldies of all
time!
     Well, Leo, every one in Euphoria is suffer-

ing from these ferocious, tired-less Grasshoppers,
and nearly having nervous brakedowns. They are de-
vowering all our beautiful plants, roses, shrubs
and even vegetables! We have all wrecked our brains
to no effect, trying different ideas of sprays and
poison and even smoke, until I had a brain-storm and
exclaimed to Herm, "Lover, if <u>anyone</u> can give us a
quick answer about the right Expert to consult in
Washington or Illinois (and to heck with expense!)
—it is Leo!"

And Hermie at once agreed, "Honey, you
have said a mouthful!"

So please do not employ your funny bone on
this one, Leo. These disgustful Grasshoppers will
eat us all out of our House and Homes at this rate if
we just stand around and allow them.

<u>Merci mille!</u>
Your friend

"Flo"

P.S. Do you yourself happen to know how to murder
Grasshoppers? Maybe we don't need a govt. "expert,"
who is probably just some politicians' dumb <u>neveu</u> in
Washington or Springfield (Ill.) having no real
<u>expertise apropos</u> agriculture and its many pests!

LEO ROSTEN
<u>Etymologist Par Excellence</u>
Katydid Concourse
Knob Lick,
Kentucky

July 10

<u>Très Cher "Flo"</u>:

You have come to the right man. It happens
that I have spent twenty-six years studying the
care and murder of grasshoppers. I may even say,
without boasting, that I am regarded as an expert
by the grasshoppers themselves, who voted me Mantis
of the Year in 1970.

Let us take the problem step-by-step, Flo.
First, are you sure that the insects who are plaguing
Euphoria are real grasshoppers? They could be
caterpillars, leaf-munchers, or even worms who
have run out of grub.

A simple test, which you ought to apply as
soon as possible, will tell you whether your pets
are really grasshoppers or one of their many imita-
tors, such as crickets. The test involves hopping
(I mean their hopping, not yours).

The common grasshopper can jump very far!
This is all the more remarkable if you consider
that grasshoppers belong to the insect order called
<u>Orthoptera</u>, which means they must often fly to an
orthopedist. Grasshoppers tend to have weak arches
and flat feet. (The same is true, of course, of many
orthopedists.) This is not true of other leaf-

eaters. Check the feet and arches of your insects.

Actually, the type of pest which creates the kind of devastation you describe is not a grasshopper but a "Migratory Locust," and belongs to the genus Melanoplus.

Now, the best way to exterminate the genus Melanoplus is to remove all over-sized watermelons from the vicinity. Replace them with footballs. Since members of the Melanoplus genus are far from being geniuses (which is why they are so crazy about watermelons in the first place), and are quite near-sighted, they cannot tell the difference between a football and a watermelon, even when their lives depend upon it. They will pounce upon every football in sight, sucking away like mad; but in a few minutes they realize, from the taste, that they are eating pigskin, and retreat in horror. It is not generally realized that after the locusts did what they did to the Hebrews, they were so overcome by guilt that they converted to Judaism. For over 40 centuries, in consequence, they have observed the kosher laws.

If you cover all lawns and backyards in Euphoria with footballs (which I admit is a costly enterprise, but well worth it) the grasshoppers, maddened by hunger, will fly away. They will search for food that meets orthodox dietary requirements even if they have to go all the way to Moskowitz and Lupowitz's in New York. Grasshoppers stop at nothing where their religious principles are involved.

The people in Gallatin, Missouri, have kept footballs around their backyards ever since their great plague of 1908, and have had so little trouble with grasshoppers of any genus, ever since, that they are the envy of gardeners throughout the Western Hemisphere. Of course, few things will grow

under the footballs, except moss, but the folks
in Gallatin prefer moss to a plague of grasshoppers.
I, for one, do not blame them.

  Let me know what happens.

       Your <u>très cher ami,</u>

        Leo

Cinderella LAMINATED SHIMS
83 Wacker Drive
Chicago, Illinois 60612

July 13

Leo Rosten
Apt. 39-A
Vesuvius Towers
644 East 68th St.
New York, N.Y.

Dear Leo:

For Chrissake, Leo! What kind of answer
was that you wrote to Flo about Grasshoppers???!
She told you how we have a plage of these G-- d---
insects and all face a real crisis—and you get on
your Yo-Yo again!

Ce-ripes, Leo, our son Alvin can do better
than that! As you will see from the enclosed, which
is a note he sent his mother Flo and I (after hearing
about the grasshoppers) from Camp Medusa, where
he is for the 4th summer in a row now.

What it boils down to I guess is that you
writers are too much of the New York type to under-

stand what a Plage of Grasshoppers can do to country folk like us!

Your pal, but disgusted—

"Herm"

P.S. Be sure to return Alvin's letter.

CAMP MEDUSA

Recreation Hall
Menomenee Knee
Wisconsin

(ENCLOSURE)

July 13

Dear Mom and Dad—

    I asked our Nature Councilor about your
Grasshopers and their ways—especially how to kill
them. He said to get a Electronic machine you can buy
at a modern Farm Supply store which sends out Ultra-
sonic sounds you and Mom would not even hear but
drives any Grasshoper bananas!
    I know it sounds freaky—but Mr. Nate
Sossnik (our Nature Councilor) has no cents of
humor so he could not be making it up. He even says
Grasshopers make those buzzing noises by rubbing
their back legs together! The Ultra-sonical buzzes
confuze them so bad that they move to another neighborhood. This is just an idea.
    Please send money.

                        Love,

                    Al (your son)

Consultant in Etymology
Tithonus Boul.
Cicada
Arizona

July 19

Herman Klitcher
Cinderella Laminated Shims, Inc.
   (Grasshopper Division)
83 Wacker Drive
Chicago, Ill. 60612

Dear Herm:

     You hurt my feelings. Apparently you do not
realize that no one sympathizes with grasshopper
plaguees more than a N.Y. writer does. Authors suf-
fer the most serious financial losses from plagia-
rism. Grasshoppers, mind you, are more decent about
this than asps. Those creatures have stolen so many
writers blind that many a new novelist doesn't know
when he is writing asp-backwards.
     Now, for the letter Alvin sent you. I hate to
say this, Herm, but that boy sounds pretty naive
to me. If I were you, I wouldn't let any child of mine
come within ten feet of a Nature Counsellor like
Nate Sossnick. Camp Medusa may be a better place
for snakes than it is for grasshoppers.
     The idea that grasshoppers make their buzz-
ing sounds by rubbing their back legs together (the
process technically known as stridulation) is one

of the most ridiculous, prejudiced misconceptions with which grasshoppers have had to contend down the centuries. That canard began in China, by some sharpshooter who palmed off 5,000 grasshoppers to a war-lord who was hard of hearing and had ordered 5,000 crickets for his forthcoming wedding. (As you know, crickets are great household pets in China, because they are believed to bring good luck, whereas grasshoppers are eaten and scorned because they symbolize the arrival of Commodore Perry's fleet.)

So much for history. Let's get back to your problem.

Modern etymologists agree to a man that grasshoppers make those grating, buzz-buzz noises not by rubbing their back legs together (tell Alvin to try that himself and see where it gets him) but by blowing on tiny kazoos, which are concealed under their wings. The male makes the "Bzz" sound and the female makes the "Zzz" reply. (Drowsy male grasshoppers often lie around snoring "Bzzzzz"—which drives the females, who reply "Zzzzzz," up the wall. I think you will agree, Herm, that nothing so infuriates a female in heat as a male who is snoozing.)

Sometimes a grasshopper produces <u>both</u> a "Bzz" and a "Zzz" sound, but in reverse—that is as "Zzz-Bzz-Zzz." This should not destroy your faith in Mother Nature. Tell Flo that if she hears that "Zzz-Bzz-Zzz" sound, it means she is listening to a neurotic Grasshopper who, because of a childhood trauma, still wets his bed.

What causes such traumas? Frankly, Herm, expert opinion is divided on this point. Etymologists who are psycho-analytically-oriented stress the harmful effects of a strict father among the <u>Orthoptera</u>; psychoanalysts in the Orient itself,

however, are inclined to blame bound feet. A third
school puts the blame squarely on damp freckles. A
grasshopper whose childhood was ruined by damp
freckles will develop all sorts of behavior problems. I have known some to end up with the D.D.T.s.

I certainly would not try to treat such a
case myself, Herm. Take the neurotic Grasshopper
to a friendly but reputable psychiatrist. (I know
this represents a problem: friendly psychiatrists
are often out of town, and reputable ones are rarely
friendly.) Psychiatrists have scored some stunning
successes in curing bed-wetting among Grasshoppers. There is only one catch, Herm. To cure
eneuresis it is necessary to get the patient to stop
jumping around so much. All that hopping up and
down not only vitiates the therapy but, worse, in-
creases the frequency of the bed-wetting.

Your friend,

Leo

P.S. Tell Alvin to ask Mr. Sossnick if he ever read
the classic work on the subject: Hoppers in the
Grass, Alas. It was written by Zertrude Ztein, one
of the few women in the fine arts whom Picasso never
made a pass at.

**From the Desk of
Herman P. Klitcher**

July 22

Dear Leo:

    All I can say is Holy Mackeral I am sorry
Flo ever even brought the subject up!

                Your buddy,

                  "Herm"

P.S. The grasshoppers are all gone, thank GOD!!!

From the
Desk
of
LEO ROSTEN

Dear Desk:

What did I tell you?

Yours,

— GOD

"Did I
Do
Wrong?"

                    Mildred J. Klitcher
                    210 Placebo Park
                    Euphoria
                    Illinois, 60035

                                              Aug. 3

Mr Leo Rostan
39-A
Vesuvio Towers
644 E. 68 Street
New York, N.Y. 10021

Dear Mr. Rostan:

        My parents Mr. and Mrs. Herman P. Klitcher
talk about you so much that whenever we have a spat
one or the other of them is prone to inform me: "And
I will bet you that Mr. Leo Rostan agrees!!" Or
sometimes "And you can even write Mr. Leo Rostan
and ask him if I (or "your father" or "your mother"
as the case may be) is not right!"
        So you see how high up on their esteam you
fit! (I think your made-up titels and addreses are
best of all.)
        Well, I am now going to take the bit into
my own teeth and without telling either one of
them (my parents) I am writing direct with a problem
I need your advice on. Which is: Why do my parents
treat me like I am a child?
        Last Saturday night they really got on
my back! They came home around 11:45 after taking
in the Tent Show of Deerfields nearby production

of "All's Swell That Ends Swell" (by Wm. Shake-
speare). And they found me not at home—which I did
not arrive at until 2:15.

Well, zap! The jazz they began to yak-yak-
yak at me—with flak about "You-should-be-ashamed-
of-yourself!" and "What-kind-of-girl-have-we-
raised-here-anyway?" and "Have-you-no-respect-
for-your-own-standards-or-ours-at-lease?" And
so on and on as if I was a nerd and am ready to throw
up! Just because I got home 2:15.

Do you, Mr. Leo Rostan, think I did wrong?

Your friend,

Miss Mildred J. Klotchn

LEON ROSTAND
c/o Ann Landers
707 Sagacity Walk
Sagatuck
Spain

Aug.7

Dear Miss Klitcher:

I can't tell until I know what you did.

Yours,

Leon Rostand

The Great
Barbecue
Contest

Cinderella LAMINATED SHIMS
83 Wacker Drive
Chicago, Illinois 60612

August 14

Leo Rosten
Apt. 39-A
Vesuvius Towers
644 E 68 St.
New York, N.Y. 10021

Dear Leo:

As you can see by the date above we are in
the middle of the Annual Sun-stroke Season. Hot ???!
Man, you can see the tar bubbling in the street the
way we used to in the old days on the West Side,
where wise-crackers like "Bobo" Blattberg used
to say it got "hotter than the hinges of H---!"
We have had 5 days in a row here where the thremo-
meter never made it below 92—and if that isn't
frying I sure would like to know what is! You can
see the spit sizzling on the sidewalks, which takes
up most of the time of all the kids in Euphoria.
So, these are nights all of us go in for
eating Out-of-doors, and the men barbecue. Ditto
me. Between the heat of the charcoal and the bitings
of blood-thirsted Mosquitos, you can drop dead
from either one! I will not even mention the effect
on body and brain.
Our gang goes in for barbecueing in a big

way, and we have some pretty big Show-offs in this
department—with fancy grills, domes, Induce
Draft Blowers, raise or low the Grill with a crank,
and etc. I still use a plain old-fashioned job, and
you can ask anyone in this neck of the woods if he
or she ever ate a better Steak, Frank, or Hamburger!!
I do not "gussy them up" with fancy Sauces the way
some of the other guys do—which makes you wonder
if they are on the sauce as well as ladeling it out.
(If you know what I mean.)

Take "Arson" Chamish, who lives 5-6 houses
down the road. "Arson" is not his real name ("Ar-
thur") but every one calls him Arson since the time he
made such a bonfire in his Barbecue that he burned the
whole 20-foot awning over his patio plus a hole
in "Nippy" Slopus roof next door. We had to call
out 3 Fire Engine Co.s before they could drench
the house on the other side—"Jo-Jo" Beaglehowl
—a mansion that cost 150,000 grand to build and
it reminds you of the Dodge Mahal. (It was Jo-Jos
wedding gift to Sandra, a goody 2 Shoes type, but
she left him 8 months later—by running away with
the bum in the Sterling Realty office who sold Jo-Jo
the lot.)

To get back to Arson Chamish. He has been
bragging all over the place about a secret Recippe
he got from a French "chef" in Paris during his 21
Day Special Tour to 10 capitols in Europe—for
barbecueing Fish! This started a real rumpus, with
the majority of us saying Fish is one thing should
never be Barbecued. Or the only time they tried,
the Fish was too dry to enjoy it.

Well, 1 word led to another until Jo-Jo
(who can hit the bottle like Willie Mays can wallop
the horeshide) offers a $500 Prize Fish-Barbecue
Contest for Labor Day!

The idea is, Jo-Jo will have 10 Barbecue
Grills lined up (and he will provide all the Fish).
3 Judges will taste the results and dish out the
prizes, which are $300 for 1st place, $100 for 2nd
place, $50 at 3rd and 4th each (which equals 500).

The Judges of the Contest who Jo-Jo picked
out are—

1) Judge Myron G. Fleischaker (of Municipal
Court here, and a dummy if you ever saw one)

2) Mrs. Geraldine ("Jerry") Winnaker who
married our local Vet (cats and dogs, no horses)

3) Helmut Andresen (thats how he spells
it, running the Universe TV-&-Hi-Fi Store here)
and his-self a real <u>darb</u> in Barbecue.

That show-off Arson Chamish is bragging he
will be the Winner—in spades!—thru his secret
French "chefs" recippe!

So this is why Im sending you this epistle,
Air Mail Spec. Delivery. On the Q.T., Leo, <u>I have
never b.b.d a Fish in my life!</u> I was groaning about
my luck in this regard when Flo had the idea of saying
"I bet your friend Leo knows the top Gourmay cooks
in N.Y. and if 1 of them can't come up with a Fish
recippe that will top Arsons and nock the Judges
eyes out, who can?!"

Thats Flo—never at a lost for an idea.

So, buddy boy, now its up to you!! RUSH me
a recippe. I do not care what <u>type</u> fish it is (to
b.b.) as Jo-Jo agrees he will supply any type each
enterant desires. Tell me what type to prefer.

My plan is—I will <u>practise in secret in
my own yard</u> and will try the results out on my own
kids and kin before the Labor Day Contest (which
is 2 weeks away). In that way, my chances can improve
sky-hi. Right?

I cant wait to see the expression on Arson Chamishs puss when he tastes my entry!!

Your old pal,

"Herm"

P.S. If I come in 1st or even 2nd all the credit will go to you, as Flo will announce it! That is her own idea, so you see there is no fly in the ointment of why I hope you have the pleasure of meeting her real soon!

LEO ROSTEN
<u>Cordon Noir</u>
School of Haute Cuisine
(Barbecue Division)
926 Alimentary Canal
Fort Lauderdale
North Dakota

Aug. 17

AIR MAIL
SPECIAL DELIVERY

Herman P. Klitcher
210 Placebo Park
Euphoria, Ill. 60035

Dear "Herm":

 Although I cannot say I ever barbecued
a 20-foot awning, I may say, in all modesty, that
you and Flo have come to the right man. My gustato-
rial masterpieces, as they are called in the fancy
restaurants of New York, where you can eat like a
King (Kong) for less that $170 per person if you
know your way around, are applauded far and wide
by those who appreciate <u>hot cuisine.</u>

 I hope that my recipe for barbecuing a fish
will help you beat "Arson" Chamish to those 300
bucks. Here is the way to do it:

 1) My marinade, which should be prepared
in advance, consists of ¼ cup of catsup, 2 oz. of

Olive Oil, 2 oz. of patchouli, 3 oz. of white wine
(a Montrachet is nifty), a touch of nutmeg, and
several sprigs of chopped parsley (fresh parsley,
Herm, not those specks from old pool-table covers).

Let the fish soak in the marinade all night
(before your contest). Salt and pepper to taste;
I don't mean taste the salt and pepper, which any
idiot can do, but add a _je ne sais quoi_ element to the
marinade. (Flo can help you viz-a-viz the _je ne sais
quoi._)

2) Prepare your fire—a 3" deep bed of teak-
wood. (I realize this is expensive, but it will
impress the hell out of the judges; tell them you
import it from Malaya—and see where Arson Chamish's
jaw drops when he hears _that!_)

3) Light your fire. This is crucial, Herm,
because cold teak will give you the jim-jams. (You
must remember that teak comes from a tropical climate and hates to change tropics.)

4) While your "bed" is getting up heat (I
mean the barbecue bed, not the one you and Flo sleep
in) rub your grille vigorously with a brush dipped
in Betel Nut juice—and jump back, because the
damn stuff sputters like mad.

5) Remove the fish from the marinade, drain-
ing off the _je ne sais quoi._

6) As soon as the spattering and sputtering
on the grille have died down, jump back towards it
and place the Fish on the grille. Note the exact
time you do this. Fish have such a subtle, delicate
taste (unlike coarse meats such as hamburger or
abalone) that one minute too long on the grille
makes a fish turn blue—whereas if you remove a
fish a half-minute too _soon,_ it will resent it and
offend your palate. (Always keep your palate in
tip-top condition, as Renoir did.

7) <u>Time the fish,</u> on the grille, giving it exactly 2½ min., then flip it over (the fish, not the grille) and give it another 2½ minutes.

8) Now comes the most important part, Herm. Using a spatula, slide the fish off the grille (do not lift it)—right off the grille and into a pail, which you had set next to the grille beforehand.

9) Place a 3-4" steak on the grill and barbecue. (I prefer mine charred on the outside and Matisse pink on the inside.)

The greatest chefs in France agree that nothing makes a steak taste better than having it replace the barbecued fish you thought you were going to have to eat.

Your old pal,

Leo

P.S. Good luck with the prize money.

**From the Desk of
Herman P. Klitcher**

Sept. 9

Dear Laughing Boy:

    I will never write you another missive
again! That is final!

                       "Herm"

From
The Desk
of
Leo Rosten

Dear Desk of Herman P. Klitcher:

    Thank you.

           —Desk of Leo Rosten

HERMAN P. KLITCHER
210 Placebo Park
Euphoria, Ill. 60035

Sept. 14

Leo Rosten
Apt. 39-A
Vesuvius Towers
644 E. 68 St.
New York, N.Y. 10021

Dear So-Call Barbecue Expert:

Are you not even <u>interested</u> to hear what
happened at the Labor Day B.B. Contest at "Jo-Jo"
Beaglehowls?? Aside from "Jo-Jo" getting stoned?

Who do you think those cockamamy Judges
handed the #1 Prize of 300 smackers to? Monty O.
Nayfish! And his barbecued perch (or whatever the
H--- it was) tasted pretty hairy to me.

And who do you think won 100 clams for being
#2? Arson Chamish! With an entry that tasted like
it came out of the Chemistry Lab at Shimmel Hi after
some years of being exhibitted as a Fossill.

Flo is just furrious about the whole thing!
She says Monty O. or Arson must of bribed the Judges,
but if you ask me the real reason is that Arson has
been getting into the "sack" since June with Mrs.
"Jerry" Winnaker—who, being a woman, probly made

the other 2 Judges vote her way! I would not be
surprised if she "made" them in both meanings of
that word! (Bob Winnaker is on the road a lot.)
    Ce-<u>ripes</u>, Leo, you cant even trust your
friends and neighbors anymore!

                              "Herm"

LEO ROSTEN
<u>American Civil Liberties Union</u>
Peter Zenger Plaza
Philadelphia
R.I.

Herman P. Klitcher
210 Placebo Park
Euphoria
Illinois

Dear "Herm":

    Where did your entry come in?

                Yours,

                Leo

HERMAN P. KLITCHER
210 Placebo Park
Euphoria, Ill. 60035

Dear Fair-Wether Friend:

My entry (stripped bass) came in # 9.

"Herm"

P.S. Maybe that was because I did not put enough
je ne sais quo in the marinade. But how could I???
I asked Flo 3 times what je ne sais quoi is and she
replied "I do not know."

Is this
an Objet
d'Art?

October 5

Dear <u>cher</u> Leo—

Since you have been a true-blue friend
in need (sometimes), I will ask you a little favor
that won't take up more than 1-2 minutes of your
time (and don't think for 1 sec I am the last to
recognize how valuabel that must really be!! <u>Pas
moi, monsieur!</u>)

I want your honest opinion of my daughter
"Baby" as an Art Talent! (She is Hermie's daughter,
also, of course, but it's natural for a mother to
say things like "my home" or "my china pattern"
or even "my son" when in fact they are owned in
common with a hubby or wife as the case may be.)

"Baby" (that is Hortense's nick-name)
is only 12, but has always been precotious, especialy in regards crayoning, finger-painting,
colors, etc. even in her nursery school days! So
I enclose a beautifull drawing she has made, for
you to have something to go by. It is a "portrait"
of Alvin, her brother, and it was done without any
hints or coxing on his or my part what-so-ever.

I think "Baby" has the possible makings
of a real <u>artiste.</u> Do you not?! In your opinion, is
this an <u>object de arts?</u>

Please do not tell Hermie I am writing—
because his nose is out of the joint, fearing I will
send Hortense to Art School after classes, which
means extra tuition, of which he complains he pays
enough already to feed 1,000 hungry children in
Indiana.

With beaucoup thanks before I get your
reply,

Toujours yours,

Florence ("Flo") K.

P.S. I enclose the picture "Baby" drew of Alvin.
Please return it after enjoying.

Leo Rosten
Apt. 39-A
Vesuvius Towers
644 E. 68 St.
New York, N.Y. 10021

LEO ROSTEN
Connoisseur: Fine Arts and Fines Herbs
149 Beret Boulevard
Left Bank
Paris, France

October 8

Dear "Flo"—

It took but a cursory examination of the
drawing you sent (which I am happy to return) for
me to conclude, reluctantly, that Hortense does
not have the makings of a real artist. I think she
has the makings of a real ornithologist.

Frankly, Flo, I have rarely seen a more
sensitive rendition of the Andalusian Thatched
Warbler. Of course (I hope you will take this in
the right spirit) if—and I stress the "if"—Alvin
happens to resemble an Andalusian Thatched Warbler
(which is nothing to scoff at; after all, Einstein
resembled a French Poodle) then I will be the first
to say that "Baby" has the makings of a superb portrait painter. In order to do this, of course, I
would have to compare her drawing of Alvin to a
photograph (of Alvin).

But you had better wait with that, Flo,
because I am just leaving for the Olduvai Gorge.
I want to see what is so new about it.

Yours,

Leo

Mrs. Herman P Klitcher
210 Placebo Park
Euphoria, Ill. 60035

From the Desk of
Herman P. Klitcher

Dear Leo:

     You really upset "Flo" (and me, too, Mac)
by using such swearing language in your epistle as
"cursory".
     There was no reason to use oats in front
of a Lady!
     Please explain your lack of being sensitive
to a womans finer feelings.

"Herm"

LEO ROSTEN
Correspondent with Furniture
48 Roller Drawer Ave.
Sheboygan
Minn.

October 12

Dear Desk:

Please extend my heartfelt apologies to
Flo. Assure her that "cursory" does not come from
"cursing" and has nothing whatsoever to do with
oaths.

"Cursory" comes from the Hindu word "curry"
and the Nepalese "sory." The combination of "curry"
(a Hindu condiment) and "sory" (a Nepalese sponge)
is one of the finest compliments a man can pay a
virgin in the Middle East.

Your pal,

Leo

**From the Desk of
Herman P. Klitcher**

Dear Leo—

     Flo and me have produced 4 children, so
how the h--- can she be a virgin??!

                              "*Herm*"

From the
Desk
of
Leo Rosten

Oct. 18

Dear Desk:

    I was talking about "Baby."

Leo

**From the Desk of
Herman P. Klitcher**

Dear Leo—

      O I see. You are right. "Baby" certainly
is "cursory."

                              "Herm"

P.S. I wish I could say the same of Penelope. "Penny"
has been dating a new string of male pistols, and
they make her former boy-friends look like "Goody-
2 Shoes." Some of them wear beards and Apache
head-ake bands and they look like fujitives from
a chain (smoking) gang! I will not let my-self even
speculate on what they are smoking, but I sure
know what they mean these days when they say someone is "freaking out" or on a "trip." They are <u>all</u>
freaks, and they never take a vacation, being on
that all year around.
      Ce-<u>ripes,</u> Leo, "going to pot" isnt what
we used to mean back on the old West Side.

                              "H"

My
Favorite
Humor-ist

MILDRED KLITCHER

Nov. 4

Hi, Mr. R!!!

    I and two other friends of mine are not
sure for who to vote (in English class) as being
our favorite humor-ist in the U.S.A. today,
        Can you help? (Ha, ha.)

        Your admirer,

        Mildred ("Pidge") K.

<u>CHIT-CHAT BING-BANG</u>
from
<u>LEO ROSTEN</u>

Nov. 11

Dear "Pidge":

    Whom are your friends? Your favorite humor-
ist may be right there among-st you.

                Your hero,

                Mr. R—

Scorched
Eggs

HORTENSE

Dec. 1

Dear Mister R—

    In my Home Econ. Class our teacher (Mrs. Oliphant) bugs me <u>blind</u> because of the way I do Eggs in class—wether fry, once-over, or any other way beside boiled.

    What she says is "Hortense Klitcher—can you tell me <u>why</u> in spite of <u>all</u> my instructing— your eggs (wether fry, over, or any other way except boiled) always come out brown and lather-y on the bottom!" (I mean lather-y like a belt or purse, Mr. R! not shaving type of lather).

    I think the stove that old Oliphant has asign me stinks. It does not work on Med. but only on Hi & Lo, but still she says it is my fault in re their timing! I have <u>loaded</u> my pan with butter or

marjorie, but still my eggs come out burnt, or
scortched on the bottom. How can I stop this??

Your friend

Hortense Clotcher

P.S. I just <u>hate</u> Mrs. Oliphant.

LEO ROSTEN
Chef des Oeufs
Yolk Drive
Shell City
Arkansas

Dec. 7

Dear Hortense:

You really would be wiser to ask your mother
about your eggs. I am certain she is an excellent
cook, whereas I am all-Tums in a kitchen.

But your plea is so affecting, and I would
so like to help, that after careful thought I came
up with an idea which just might help you. To avoid
scorching eggs so that they do not get all brown
and lathery on the bottom, I would reverse the
position of the eggs as I pour them into the pan.
This will put what used to be the bottom up on top.
Therefore (if my reasoning is correct), I would
no longer get brown leathery bottoms, but brown,
leathery tops, which happen to be the height of
fashion this year.

Your friend,

Mr. R—

P.S. I hate Mrs. Oliphant, too.

The Disappearance
of an
Author

Cinderella LAMINATED SHIMS
83 Wacker Drive
Chicago, Illinois 60612

Dec. 12

Leo Rosten
Apt. 39-A
Vesuvius Towers
644 E. 68 St.
New York, N.Y. 10021

Dear Leo:

Get set, kiddo! <u>Great</u> news! And dont pass
out in front of your eyes!

Right after Shimmel Hi lets out for Xmas
the Klitcher tribe are coming to New York!! (Just
to visit, not move—as it sure beats me why people
want to live there!)

I dont have to tell you what a <u>thrill</u> this
is going to be for the kids, never having seen the
Big City before—tho I took 1 trip in 1963 with Flo
(who you will at last have the pleasure of meeting)!

We will drive all the way. And you won't
hardly beleive this, I bet, but except for the Stop
Light right here in Euphoria, and the other before
the Eden Expressway, we can ride <u>all the way</u> allmost
1,000 miles to the George W. Bridge across the Hudson
River without hitting even 1 other! Hows <u>that</u> for
progress in your Sister City of Chi.??!

Now about our visit. I dont want you to nock yourself out for us, Leo, for the 5 days we expect to be "living things up" in Manhattan! Just meeting you for a get-together at some famous Restaurent will give Flo and the kids a real kick!

We expect to leave here on Dec. 18 A.M. and arrive on Dec. 20 (around 5 P.M.) and go right to the King Arthurs Court Motel—to who my new Sec. wrote 10 days ago for reservations. (You just have to see this squirrel to beleive her! Her wits, if any, are dim. Her name is Daphne Hunziger and she is more daffy than Daphne. She has a fobia about Germs, as she keeps calling the Board of Health every hour to hear "the pollen count," tho I have yet to hear her sneeze.)

I told Daphne to be sure and follow up on the reservation, as we need 4 double rooms. Can you tie that? We have to have 4 doubles—on account of having 3 daughters and only 1 son, where if we insted had 2 girls and 2 boys we could do it with 3 doubles (me and Flo having our own room apart from the others.) I have told Daphne to re-confirm.

So get set, pal, and roll out the screamers! The Klitchers are coming to town!!!

Your buddy,

"Herm"

P.S. Could you just make a list of Main Attractions in N.Y. which are musts for us not to miss? Like Shows on Broadway, and should we bother going up to the top of the Empire State (now that we have the Sears

highest build. in the World right here in Chi!).
Also a few French-type restaurants that dont charge
you an arm-and-leg for fancy table-clothes plus
a Metro d. who bows you in and expects a buck for
each bow.

So, buckel your seat belt, pal. See you
soon—with bells on! <u>Here we come!!</u>

H

Flo wants to pitch in her best wishes.

P.P.S. <u>Cher</u> Leo:

I am just as excited as Herm! As Mark Laf-
ayett said, "Leo, <u>nous arriverons!</u>"

<u>Votre ami,</u>

"Flo"

Sophie Cassandra
Secretary to Leo Rosten
Vesuvius Towers
644 E. 68 St.
New York, N.Y. 10021

December 14

Mr. & Mrs. Herman P. Klitcher
210 Placebo Park
Euphoria, Illinois, 60035

Dear Mr. and Mrs. Klitcher:

     Mr. Rosten was flown to Switzerland this morning on orders from his doctor, who (in fact) took him there. No one knows how long Mr. Rosten will be confined.

     I am forwarding your letter to the Director of the <u>Allgemeiner Krankenhaus</u> in Gstaad. It may throw light on Mr. Rosten's strange seizure.

Yours truly,

Sophie Cassandra

Secretary

Internationale Allgemeiner Krankenhaus
43-49 Korsakoff Syndrome
Gstaad
Gswitzerland

L'Office du Directeur
Oscar Pflaumenbrenner, M.D.

December 17

Herr & Frau Herman P. Klitcher
210 Placebo Park
Euphoria, Illinois 60035

My dear Herr und Frau Klitcher:

Gratings!
Your letter to Herr Leo Rosten was forward
sent to us by Fraulein Sophie Cassandra, former
secretary to our valuable patient. (She has dis-
appeart.)
Herr Rosten has been diagnosed as "sick."
He is a chronic M.D.. Treatment for these Manic
Depressive phases has begun to begin.
The prognosis is 50-50. Do not expect him
to return to New York for some time.
I am begging you to remain,

Oscar Pflaumenbrenner

Directeur

P.S. Would you be so kind to enform me when you
arrive back home in Euphoria, Illinois?

Back home from Gstaad (Gswitzerland), where his
manic depression cleared up the very day he learned
that the Herman Klitchers had returned to Euphoria,
Illinois, Leo Rosten is clinging to his unlisted
telephone number and a solemn vow never to cor-
respond with old school chums again.

If Dear "Herm" seems a startling venture
for a man who is a Ph.D. from the University of
Chicago, has been a distinguished visiting pro-
fessor of Political Science at the University of
California, and has written the definitive Leo
Rosten's Treasury of Jewish Quotations, it should
be remembered that he created immortal hilarity
with The Education of H* Y* M* A* N K* A* P* L* A* N,
The Joys of Yiddish, Captain Newman, M.D., and People
I Have Loved, Known or Admired.